Nelly

W9-AHF-968

# MOUNTAIN
# SOLO

ALSO BY JEANETTE INGOLD

*The Big Burn*

*Airfield*

*Pictures, 1918*

*The Window*

# MOUNTAIN SOLO

*Jeanette Ingold*

Harcourt, Inc.

ORLANDO   AUSTIN   NEW YORK
SAN DIEGO   TORONTO   LONDON

www.HarcourtBooks.com

This is a work of fiction. Any resemblance of the characters to
actual people, living or dead, is purely coincidental.

Library of Congress Cataloging-in-Publication Data
Ingold, Jeanette.
Mountain solo/Jeanette Ingold.
p    cm.
Summary: Back at her childhood home in Missoula, Montana,
after a disastrous concert in Germany, a teenage violin prodigy
contemplates giving up life with her mother in New York City and her
music as she, her father, stepmother, and stepsister hike to a pioneer
homesite where another violinist once faced difficult decisions of his own.
[1. Violinists—Fiction. 2. Family life—Montana—Fiction. 3. Mothers and
daughters—Fiction. 4. Stepfamilies—Fiction. 5. Frontier and pioneer life—
Montana—Fiction. 6. Schools—Fiction. 7. Montana—Fiction.]   I. Title.
PZ7.I533Mo   2004
[Fic]—dc21    2003042326
ISBN 0-15-202670-3

Designed by Lydia D'moch
Printed in the United States of America

C  E  G  H  F  D  B

For my daughter, Carie

# MOUNTAIN SOLO

# TESS & FREDERIK

# TESS

M om, stop!" I said, as she smoothed my hair and reminded me not to rush the opening bars of my solo. I took a deep breath and walked quickly onto the stage.

And then I turned, and a spotlight came on so bright that I took a step back from it. My whole body seemed to go numb, and when the applause that had greeted me ended, my head felt squeezed by the silence.

"*Fräulein?*" the conductor whispered.

I nodded automatically. *Yes, I am ready.*

But I wasn't.

From the corner of my eye, I saw his baton's upbeat set a tempo and then swoop low, and behind me the orchestra's strings swept into the beginning measures of a Vivaldi concerto.

I raised my violin and fixed in my mind how my first notes should sound. I would play them just the way I had when I'd won the young artists competition that brought me here to Germany.

*One more measure . . . there . . . Now!*

I pulled my bow in a quick downstroke and heard a discordant tone tear out raw and wrong.

That's what I keep remembering. How once I'd played that note so badly, there was no way to get it back. And how that one mistake led to another and another—a missed accent, a hurried rest beat, an odd angle to my bow arm. One off note after another, after another, after another.

Somehow my hands, on their own, played to the concerto's end: played decently through the easy parts when I should have been preparing for the trouble spots and wasn't; faltered through the hard sections with only what my fingers remembered and nothing of what I needed to add from my head and my heart.

When the orchestra finally stopped playing and I turned back to the conductor, I couldn't meet his eyes.

"Well, *fräulein,*" he said. "So."

# FREDERIK

1905

F rederik Bottner stared out at South Dakota farmland
that looked as lonely as he felt and wished he had
his parents to decide for him. Although if he still had his
parents, he wouldn't be facing this decision at all. Uncle
Conrad, who was a professor of music in Germany,
wouldn't have written him, and Uncle Joe...

Frederik remembered how his parents had smiled
when Uncle Johann's first letter from his new home in
Montana arrived last January. How they laughed at the way
he signed his name "Joe" and shook their heads at how he
urged them farther west to take up a place near him.

He wrote, "I've found a mountain valley where trees
scent the air like in the old country, and wind doesn't
sand away a body's skin."

Leave South Dakota? they asked. Where they had so
much? They were used to the wind.

The letter stayed on the table for days, though, drawing Frederik's eyes and setting him to dreaming about

mountain country while he studied or worked or practiced the violin his father had begun teaching him to play. From the start, Frederik had shown a skill that alternately pleased and frustrated his father.

"Frederik! Give attention," Heinrich Bottner would say. Then he'd adjust Frederik's hold on the instrument. "One day you're going to want to play this properly, and what if you have no one to teach you?"

"Father," Frederik asked during one of his lessons, "do you think you might ever consider moving?"

"I think you should attend to what you're doing!"

"Yes, sir," Frederik answered, but his mother took the violin and handed it to his father.

"Husband," she said, "if you want us to enjoy this, then *you* play it. Our son will learn music when he's ready." Her eyes teased. "Frederik, your father is going to play now. We must give attention!"

In Frederik's house on the harsh prairie, his father's violin playing was the one thing besides sleep that brought work to a stop. Even his mother's hands sat idle in her lap, not knitting or stitching, when his father's violin sang above the wind.

But that was last January, the first month of 1905.

In March, as snow gave way to mud and the barnyard became a quagmire of thawing manure, Frederik's mother came down with typhoid. Heinrich Bottner's violin stayed silent during his wife's last days, as he sat by her bedside endlessly repeating, *"Gott im himmel...* Dear

*Gott im himmel."* And a few months later, still preoccupied with grief, he lost his own life in a careless accident.

With the help of a church pastor, Frederik wrote his uncles of Heinrich's death. And now both had sent back invitations for Frederik to live with them.

Uncle Joe wrote, "I share your grief, nephew. But come! Montana is a fine place with a lot of opportunities for an able young man."

A pastor translated the letter Uncle Conrad sent from Munich. "I have a son who is also fourteen," Conrad Bottner wrote. "You would be company for him and me, and if you have your father's talent as a musician, I will teach you violin as I'm teaching my son."

Frederik hardly knew what to make of an uncle who, given all he could have written about, offered violin lessons. Or did Uncle Conrad guess that along with missing his family, Frederik missed the music they'd shared? Was that what he was offering? Music?

But to leave everything familiar and start an entirely different life so far away... And to go with no assurance that things would work out...

Of course Frederik wouldn't have any assurances going to Montana, either, but neither would he be running quite so far into the unknown.

He looked at the letters in his hand, wishing they could tell him if one choice or the other would be a mistake.... wondering how, and when, he would know if he chose right.

# MOUNTAIN SOLO

# TESS

My mother and I returned to New York the next day, and now, two weeks later, barely into July, I'm on a late-night plane to Montana and still burning with shame. And no closer to understanding how I could have failed.

All I know is that it will never happen again. I'm taking my violin as far away as I can from everything that put me on that stage.

My throat tightens as I hold down the tears that have been hovering this whole flight out. What if Mom's right, and at sixteen years old I'm making the biggest mistake of my life?

As the plane nears Missoula, passengers lean toward cold windows, and I recognize a moonlit summer valley an instant before someone says, "We're coming in over the Rattlesnake."

Scattered lights—one of them must be my dad's house—merge into the close-packed ones of downtown.

Not very many lights, really, and dark mountains ring the bright basin like a cord pulled tight.

The hardest thing was getting Mom to believe I was serious. "Leave your violin teacher? Drop out of music school?" *Are you crazy?* her tone implied. Then she changed arguments. "And how can you want to live with a stepfamily you haven't even met?"

I didn't know how to answer her; I never do, but for once I didn't give in, either. On my own, I had called Dad for a plane ticket and sorted my things into what I'd take with me and what I'd have sent on later.

If I have them sent on. I couldn't tell Mom I was already worrying that staying away from New York might be harder than remaining. She'd have grabbed on to a weakness like that and enlarged it until I'd be back right where she wanted me.

Now, as we angle down to the runway, I think about Mom seeing me off from La Guardia Airport earlier today.

She was so silently angry, I wasn't sure she'd even say good-bye. But she'd suddenly touched the violin case I was clutching. "At least you're taking that with you," she said, and for a brief instant she really seemed to want to understand.

I wish I could have explained. Could have offered something better, anyway, than only telling her, "I couldn't leave it behind."

Though that's the truth. I couldn't.

Dad's tall enough that I easily spot him amid the airport confusion. "Hey!" I yell, running to him for a hug. He looks so welcoming with his arms open wide that I have to fight back a sudden urge to cry. "Hey," I say, and I hang on to his neck a moment before stepping back.

His gaze shifts to a girl rapidly weaving her way through the crowd. *Amy,* I think, recognizing her from photos. Without slowing down she looks over her shoulder, hollers, "Mom, she's here!" and rams into the edge of a display case. Her mouth opens in surprise when she sees the huge grizzly bear towering inside.

I hurry over with Dad, who asks, "You all right? No permanent damage? The bear didn't bite?"

The poor kid's face is crimson with embarrassment.

"I don't see any puncture marks," I joke, hoping to make her laugh. Then I add, "I'm happy to meet you, Amy. I'm Tess."

She shoots me a mortified glance and barely mumbles a hello.

"And I'm Meg," someone says, and I turn to meet Dad's new wife. She's taller than I'd pictured; fit looking; wears her hair, black like Amy's but faded, loosely caught behind her head. She says, "We are so glad you're here, Tess."

I offer her my hand to shake, but she laughs and hugs me. A real hug, not at all like one of Mom's, which doesn't mess up hairstyles and makeup. Meg hugs as though she means it.

As WE DRIVE away from the airport, I think about how you hear that a man sometimes marries the same woman twice. The same *kind* of woman. I suppose that deep down that's what I expected Dad to have done, but my brief impression of Meg is that she's as different from Mom as comfortable jeans are from a tailored silk suit. Which is both reassuring and scary, because Mom, at least, I'm used to.

I look over at my stepsister, who's huddled in her corner of the backseat, apparently still embarrassed over her collision with the display case. I tell her, "If you moved that grizzly bear to New York, somebody would build a whole museum around it."

She makes a small noise that could be a sniff or a giggle.

I tell her, "You make the third Amy that I know. There are two in my school."

She whispers, "Dancers."

Surprised, I ask, "How did you know that?"

She shrugs, and I'm thinking there are easier things than trying to talk with a nine-year-old when suddenly she says, "We're going backpacking."

"Who?"

"Us. Day after tomorrow. Pop bought a new tent just for you and me."

*Pop?* I wonder, and then I realize she means Dad.

Amy's voice turns anxious. "Is that okay?"

"Sharing a tent? Yes, but...Dad?" I say, leaning forward. "Is that right? I was expecting to have some time—"

Amy asks, "Don't you want to go?"

"It's not that," I answer. "I'm just surprised."

Meg says, "The timing's my doing. Part of the reason we're going is to pin down the location of an old homestead site while there's still enough summer left to do a good follow-up."

For a second I don't know what she's talking about, and then I remember. She's a historian—an archaeologist, actually—with the Forest Service. I ask, "So this will be a working vacation?"

"Partly," she answers. "For me."

"Got it," I say.

I'd just as soon not get to know my new family under circumstances that throw us together every minute, but working vacations are one thing I understand. It will just be odd to watch someone else do the work.

I sleep in the guest room since Amy's taken over mine and wake up the next morning to clear sunshine and different sounds than I'm used to. Here there're no horns or sirens; there's no city roar.

The nightstand clock says 11:30—I never sleep so late!—and I realize Dad and Meg must have left for work hours ago. I listen for Amy and then remember her mentioning something about spending the day with a friend. Getting out of the unfamiliar bed, I feel oddly out of place, and the sensation grows as I go through the house, looking at it in a way that I couldn't last night. I know I've got a right to be here, but there's just enough difference from how it used to be to make me feel like an intruder.

Things I expect to see are gone, replaced by things that I don't know, like a new countertop in the bathroom. And framed pictures from the Hawaii wedding that Mom decided I shouldn't attend because, she said, I couldn't afford the time.

I pause at the doorway to Dad and Meg's room, which still has the furniture from when it was his and Mom's. It's been rearranged, though, and the patterned wallpaper and heavy drapes are gone. Now it's just dark wood, white walls, and uncovered windows looking out at trees hung with a half-dozen bird feeders.

The changes are jolting—as though I closed my eyes on the past and opened them to find it changed—and they remind me how little I know about my new step-mother. It takes effort to push down a worry that we might not get along.

When I get to my old room, though, I burst out laughing. Amy's version of leaving it neat was to pile a foot-high heap of stuff on her bed and cover it with the spread. I pick up a stray sock and shove it in with her other things.

And then I see the pictures under the glass top of her desk, and my stomach does a little flip-flop. It's a collage of photos cut from a teen magazine article about my academic school, which is just for kids who are studying to be performing artists or already have professional careers. Amy has mounted them on colored paper and used gold ink to write in our names and what we do.

I trace the faces through the glass and wonder if I'll ever see them again.

There's one of Kiah, Eleni, and both Amys in their leotards and ballet slippers. And there's me with my violin, standing next to Kendall, whom I'd just as soon *not* see again.

I find the group shot that's my favorite. Ben, my best friend in all the world, is in the middle of it, one hand supporting his cello and an expression on his face like he'd rather be playing it than posing.

Ben doesn't even know I've left New York. Besides cello, he plays a pretty good string bass, and when I got back from Germany he was already off on his summer job, touring New England with a jazz group. He called four or five times, but I let him talk to the answering machine.

Out of habit I glance at my watch and calculate the practice time left in the day. Then I remember I don't have to do that anymore. The whole afternoon and evening lie wide open, with no new music for me to learn and nothing old to polish. I can leave my violin case closed the way it has been for the past two weeks.

The sheer freedom makes me feel a little giddy.

*Or maybe I'm just hungry,* I think. *Should I have breakfast or lunch?*

In the kitchen I drink orange juice while looking at another photo. This one, which is on the refrigerator door, is of me when I was three and a half, or almost. I'm wearing a bathrobe and cradling my new violin the way I might a doll. Mom's neatly printed label has almost faded away, but I can still make it out. I was Tessie back then. Occasionally still am.

Then I spot a note from Dad propped against a cereal bowl. "I'll pick you up at lunchtime—noon sharp—so we can buy you some camping gear."

I start to hurry down the hall and then have to back-track to answer the phone.

"Tess," Mom says, "why didn't you call and tell me you'd arrived safely? Anyway, I want you to know that I've spent the entire morning straightening out the mess you left behind."

"I didn't leave a mess."

"Most importantly, I've gotten your violin teacher to understand that you're on a needed mental health break—"

*Mental health break!* "But that's not true! Why would you tell Mr. Stubner that?"

"So he'll keep a place in his schedule. I'm keeping doors open for you."

"You had no right."

"But they won't stay open forever, so don't dawdle too long in coming to your senses. And don't let up on your practicing. You don't want to get further behind than you can help."

My gaze swings to the microwave display that says 11:48. I think, *Dad will be here in twelve minutes.* Again I calculate the hours I have left in the day. It's a habit hard to break, and I feel guilty for even trying to. Or maybe the unsettled feeling inside me is dismay at how easy it would be to give in to Mom.

I know that if I stay on the phone with her, she'll soon be telling me what music to work on. And then, be-fore I know how she's made it happen, I'll be on another airplane, on my way back to New York and a life I don't want anymore.

Making my voice steady, I say, "I can't practice for several days at least because we're going on a camping trip. I'll call when we get back."

And then I hang up.

I take a fast shower, throw on some clothes, and am in the driveway pulling my hair into a ponytail when Dad drives up.

Shopping with him is a fast affair. It takes us ten minutes at one store to get a sleeping bag to replace the one I outgrew years ago—Amy will use that—and fifteen minutes at another to pick out an internal-frame pack that looks as if it will hold a lot more than I want to carry. I'm kind of stunned at the size of the checks he has to write, but he says they're part early happy birthday—my birthday's three weeks away—and part welcome-home gift.

Lunch is milkshakes and onion rings, which used to be our secret treat. Then Dad has to get back to his veterinary clinic. He tells me, "If you wouldn't mind getting a ride home with Meg, it will save me some driving."

"Isn't she working?" I ask.

"She has an appointment at a nursing home out this

way and then is taking off early to get things ready for tomorrow."

"What's she doing at a nursing home?"

"She didn't say. Just called to suggest I drop you off there."

"I'M SUPPOSED TO meet Meg Thaler," I tell a man at the front desk.

"Dr. Thaler?" he asks, and I almost say no before I remember she is one, a Ph.D. doctor. "She got here just ahead of you," he says, gesturing down a long hall.

Spotting Meg toward the far end, I hurry and catch up with her as she pauses in a doorway. She gives me a smile while speaking to someone I can't see. "Miss Bottner?" she says.

"I wanted to let you know I'm here," I whisper. "I'll wait in the lobby."

"Please stay," she tells me. "Miss Bottner?" she says again, stepping inside. "Katharina?"

Meg motions me into the room, where a woman sits at a window. Even though her back is toward us, she gives the impression of being very old. And when she reaches for the controls to make her wheelchair circle around, I see scars, darkened and puckered with age, stretching across fingers that strain to work the buttons.

Once she's facing our way, she urges, "Sit down, sit

down. And tell me who you are. Someone said, but I do forget..."

"I'm Meg Thaler," Meg says, "and this is my step-daughter, Tess."

"Well, tell her to sit, too," the woman says.

There's only one visitor's chair, so I take up a place on the floor where I can lean back against a bureau.

Meg says, "I work for the Forest Service, and one of my projects is locating the place where you grew up. It's probably the last undocumented homestead site in the Rattlesnake, and..."

Katharina Bottner listens attentively to the explanation, but when Meg says, "I was hoping you could tell me some landmarks to look out for," Katharina replies with, "Are you the girl come to give me my bath?"

Meg's cheeks turn a faint pink. "No," she says, and starts over with a simpler explanation.

Katharina interrupts to ask me, "And who are you again?"

"Tess Thaler," I say.

"And you?" she asks Meg.

"I'm Meg Thaler, from the Forest Service." Meg touches Katharina's hand, and again I notice the scars. "Katharina, it would really help me to know about where you grew up. Do you remember if your parents farmed the land?"

Sudden humor sparkles in Katharina's eyes. "They

certainly didn't run a store on it. Wouldn't have had any customers but wild animals."

Meg chuckles but pushes on. "Do you remember what buildings you had? Besides a house? A barn, perhaps?"

"Certainly we had a barn," Katharina says. "If I could, I'd ask Papa to show you." She halts, appearing puzzled, as though she's trying to pull together some thought. Then she shakes her head. "But I haven't seen him in a long time."

Meg waits a few moments, and then she says, "Your father was a violin player, wasn't he?"

"I haven't seen him in a long time," Katharina repeats. She looks down at her hands. "He would have taught me to play, you know, only of course there was the dynamite. My own fault for wandering off. I'd been told."

"Dynamite?" Meg asks as I shudder at the image of a little kid being hurt by explosives. But Katharina is done talking about it. And when Meg tries to direct the conversation back to the homestead, Katharina starts talking about the young robins outside her window.

We thank her for seeing us and are saying good-bye when the puzzled expression returns to her face. Then it dissolves as she apparently finds the thought she was after. "I do have something of Papa's you can look at."

She rolls her wheelchair to a closet, slides open the door, and nods toward a shelf crammed with bags and boxes. "It's up there," she says, looking at me. "You'll have to move some things."

Meg motions for me to go ahead, and I'm about to ask what I should be looking for when I see the unmistakable shape of a violin case. I pull it down and set it on the bed. "Your father's?" I ask.

"That's what I said," Katharina answers.

"May I open it?"

"You won't see it unless you do."

As I ease back the worn, stiff latches, Meg says, "Tess is a violinist herself."

Katharina says, "Papa called it a fiddle."

The hinges squeak when I lift the lid, and the mingled scents of rosin, old wood, and decaying fabric rush out. The violin that rests on the case's crushed-velvet lining has one peg that looks different from the others, and two of its strings are missing.

"Will you play a piece?" Katharina asks.

I draw a finger over the instrument's curved, finely crackled surface, sad to have to tell her, "I'd like to, but this isn't in any shape to play."

"Oh." The single word is soft with disappointment.

"I'm sorry," I tell her. "What kind of music did your father play?"

"Every kind you can name. Square-dance music and hymns and old-timey things like 'Go Tell Aunt Rhody.' One year when every one of our lambs lived right to market, Mama even bought him a book of music so he could learn some different pieces. That's when he learned 'Danny Boy.'" Katharina's eyes focus on a point in midair. "What I liked best, though, were his woods sounds."

"What were those?" I ask.

"Oh, just one thing and another we'd hear. Birds singing, owls, like that." Frowning, she looks at the instrument and makes a small humphing noise in her throat. "Well, put it away." She reaches for the buttons of her wheelchair. "You'd better go now. I'm tired."

We're in the hall when Katharina calls us back. "Girl," she says to me, "what's your name again?"

"Tess."

"Did you come here by train?"

"Come to...?" I hesitate, wondering if she means to the nursing home and not sure it's polite to call it that.

"To Montana, of course," she says. "Papa came by train, carrying that fiddle all the way from South Dakota."

"You were with him?"

"Why, he was just a boy. I wasn't even born!" She chuckles. "The idea!"

D id you know she had that violin?" I ask Meg as we get in her small pickup truck.

She shakes her head. "I knew her father—Frederik Bottner—played one because it was mentioned in a newspaper clipping about a dance in the old Rattlesnake schoolhouse. That's why I wanted you to meet Katharina. I thought she might have some interesting stories to tell you. But that she'd still have his violin... That was certainly unexpected."

"Her father's playing must have meant a lot for her to have kept his fiddle when she couldn't play it herself. Do you think she meant that a dynamite explosion was what ruined her hands? How would a kid have gotten hold of that?"

"In homestead days?" Meg says. "You name it. People used dynamite for blowing up tree stumps, blasting irrigation ditches, opening up mine tunnels. There were so many ways for kids to get hurt or killed back then: open fires, boiling kettles of laundry, livestock that couldn't always be trusted, wild animals."

"You make those times sound awful," I say.

"Not awful. Just hard and full of risk." She pauses. "I think an accident with dynamite would have been more likely to kill Katharina than just hurt her hands. But maybe some smaller explosive, something she associates with dynamite..."

We stop by Meg's office in the Forest Service building at old Fort Missoula, and I wait in the car while she makes a quick trip inside. She comes out carrying a folder that she gives me. "Photocopies from our Rattlesnake files," she says. "And maps. You can see on the first one where I think the Bottner home probably was."

I unfold a topographic map labeled "Rattlesnake National Recreation and Wilderness Area." A tiny black dot indicates our house just outside the boundary, and a penciled X marks the mouth of a gulch several miles in.

"That location's just an educated guess," Meg tells me, slowing for traffic backed up by road construction. "I found a 1909 land claim filed by Frederik Bottner, but most of the legal description was too water damaged to read." She breaks off to ask, "What do you think would be the fastest way to go? Reserve Street to Broadway?"

Shaking my head, I say, "Missoula's grown so much you probably know it better than I do."

I study the map. The X-marked gulch, which is narrow to start with, tapers in to become just the blue thread of a stream cutting down the contour lines of a mountainside.

Meg mutters under her breath as she slows for an asphalt truck. "I swear every road in Missoula is being worked on at the same time." She makes a sharp left. "Let's see if this is better."

As I put away the topo map, I notice a picture of a rusted-out kettle and ask what's special about it.

"That's what started this search," Meg answers. "A hiker came across it a good bit farther up the 'Snake than any of the documented homesites, which raised the question of whether there was a site we didn't know about. Then I found that land claim, and Bottner is an unusual enough name that I was able to track down Katharina."

Frowning at yet another traffic snarl, Meg detours from her detour. "Actually," she continues, "there were two Bottners who seemed to have owned land in the Rattlesnake. The other was a Johann who moved there some years before it was all officially surveyed. A relative, I assume."

Meg's revised route takes us to a brick-paved street that runs along the railroad tracks at the north end of downtown Missoula, and we stop at a crosswalk to wait for a couple of adults and a dozen little kids in day-camp T-shirts.

"Must be a field trip to engine thirteen-fifty-six," Meg says, gesturing toward a steam locomotive that's ending its days inside a fence near the old Northern Pacific depot.

Remembering what Katharina said, I suggest, "Maybe Katharina's father came in right here."

"He well could have," Meg answers. "People like to think of homesteaders arriving by covered wagon, but the truth is most of the ones who took up land out here arrived after the covered-wagon days were over."

I picture a boy in old-fashioned overalls, a farm kid from a prairie state—South Dakota, Katharina said—struggling to get his bearings at a bustling train station in an unfamiliar mountain city. "It's too bad Katharina couldn't tell us more about him," I say.

"That's one of the frustrating things about studying the past," Meg says. "You have to accept that you'll never learn all there is to know about the people who lived in it. Though of course you keep wondering."

I see what she means, because I'm wondering myself what that boy thought about as his train pulled into Missoula. Did he look out a window to see what awaited, or was he remembering what he'd left behind?

As the last stragglers reach the sidewalk, Meg shifts into first and drives forward. Out on the tracks, a brakeman waves to the engineer of an incoming freight train, and slowing boxcars rumble and boom.

M eg asks, "Home, or do you want to go grocery shopping with me?"

"Home, if you wouldn't mind," I answer. "I'd like to get unpacked."

The job doesn't take long, though, and once again I find myself wandering the house. In the living room, I see that someone's put my violin on the piano. *I ought to take it to my room,* I think, without moving toward it. I bring a cola from the kitchen, page through a magazine, and then abruptly put it down.

I go over to my violin, open the case, and run my hand over the instrument inside—the way I felt the wood of Katharina's father's violin. Plucking a couple of strings, I wince at how they've slipped out of tune.

Bringing them back up to pitch, I play a few chords, and it feels so good that I think maybe I'll keep going, just for a little while. I sound a few more chords, considering. I know so many pieces, but I think that what I *should* play is my solo. When you make a mistake, you don't go on until you fix it. At least I never have.

Only, when I try that first note, the one I last heard tear out raw and wrong into a concert hall full of people, I bow it almost too softly to be heard. *I'm scared of it,* I think. *One little note, and I'm scared of it.*

I take a deep breath, prepare to try again, and am glad when Amy's bursting through the front door gives me an excuse not to. She holds out a chalk picture of two tents in a mountain meadow. "It was arts day at the park," she says. "I made this for you."

"Thank you," I say. I start to comment on the wild, bright colors she used, but she's looking at my violin. "Can I hold it?"

"If you're careful."

I put it in both her hands, but she says, "No. Like you hold it."

So, with my hands around hers, I put it into position. "Rest your chin on that black oval piece." I help her bow some open strings, but she wants real music.

"You've got to know fingering to play a melody," I tell her. "That takes lessons and practice."

"Then you play," she says.

I hesitate, but then I think, *She's not expecting Vivaldi.* "What would you like to hear?"

"I don't know."

" 'Danny Boy,' " Meg says, pausing in the hall, sacks

of groceries in her arms. "It's been going around in my head ever since Katharina mentioned it."

"Don't you want help putting those away?" I ask.

"No, thanks. Not this time," she answers.

So, accompanied by the quiet click of kitchen cabinets being opened and shut, I play my violin for the first time since the concert. Amy watches, her arms wrapped across her middle. She's a rapt, uncritical audience, and "Danny Boy" is so lovely and simple it almost plays itself. Only, when I'm halfway through it, I can't go on.

I stop in the middle of a phrase. "I'm sorry, Amy," I say. "I'll have to play for you another time."

"Why?" she asks.

"I'm sorry," I repeat as I put my violin in its case.

There aren't any sounds from the kitchen for a few moments, and then Meg calls, "Amy, will you please come set the table?"

WE EAT DINNER in the kitchen. Supper, really, since it's just soup and sandwiches. Amy is telling a drawn-out story about her friend's little brother being a major plague when she suddenly breaks off to tell Dad, "Tess played her violin for me today. She's wonderful."

"You don't have to convince me of that," he says.

"Of course, she's been playing a long time." Amy points to the photo on the refrigerator, the one of me when I was a little kid. "Since then, right?"

"Since then," I agree. "That was taken the Christmas I got my first violin."

"Is it what you asked for?"

"I don't remember," I tell her. "I know I was happy to get it."

Dad laughs. "No, you weren't, Tess. You wanted a drum."

"No!" I protest. I know he's wrong because I can see so clearly how that long-ago day was. Mom's told me how my eyes grew big with wonder when I first saw the violin, and how I took it from its case and cradled it.

I ask, "A drum?"

"A drum," Dad answers. "A toy drum like one that a little friend of yours had."

"And I didn't want the violin?"

"Nope."

*Lenny,* I suddenly remember. That was the boy's name. His drum had one red rim and one blue.

I look again at the photo on the refrigerator. It's been there almost forever reminding me, as Mom says, how my violin and I were a match from the start. How the first note I bowed was perfect and how after hearing it I never wanted to do anything but play my violin.

Amy asks Dad, "Was it Christmas Eve or Christmas morning when Tess got her violin? Because Mom and I open presents in the morning, but if you want to do Christmas Eve, that's okay."

Meg tells her, "I don't think we need to decide that now, with Christmas still half a year away."

Dad says, "Anyway, we've always been a Christmas morning family, too. And nobody"—he gives Amy a fierce, teasing scowl that sets her giggling—"*nobody* goes in to see presents until everybody's ready."

"But how does everybody know?" Amy asks.

"Because I tell 'em!" Dad answers. "Right, Tess?"

"Right!" I say. "Right," I repeat. "Right."

# TESSIE

Hey, sleepyhead!" Dad said. "Don't you want to see what Santa's brought?"

Mom's voice came from the next room. "Stephen, it's hardly light out!"

"Tessie couldn't sleep," Dad called back. He winked at me. "Could you?"

"Did Santa come?" I asked. I scrambled up and tried to slip past the bathrobe he held out.

"Not so fast, squirt," he said. "We have to wait for your mom, anyway. Put this on and then we'll see what kind of day we've got."

He opened the curtains, and cold air blew in. A deer bounded away from a bird feeder, and I wanted it to be a reindeer even though I knew it wasn't.

"Is Santa back at the North Pole?" I asked.

"I imagine so," Dad answered. Then we heard Mom coming down the hall. "It's time!"

In the living room, Mom and Dad watched me while I hugged dolls, linked plastic building blocks, and twisted the dials on a toy stove that had tiny, real pans in its oven.

Then I remembered the toy drum I'd asked Santa for. I'd told him I wanted one just like my friend Lenny had that you could beat and march with. "Santa forgot my drum," I said.

"Maybe he brought you something better," Mom told me. "Look here."

"What is it?" I asked.

"A violin."

"What does it do?"

"It makes music."

I looked for a way to turn it on. "How?"

"Someone has to play it, of course. Pluck one of the strings."

The violin didn't make music at all. It made a tiny sound like a little *plicck* that stopped almost as soon as it started.

Wondering why she thought that was better than a drum, I went back to my toy stove.

Dad said, "I told you so."

"Tessie, wait," Mom said. "You don't understand." Pulling me to her, she put the violin against my neck. "Rest your chin here and hold it like this . . ."

I didn't like how it felt. "I don't want to. It's pinching me."

"Oh, for heaven's sake," Mom said, but she tucked

up my bathrobe collar so it was between the violin and me. "There! Now don't let go." She reached around me and steadied my grip. "I'm going to pull the bow across the strings."

That gave a better sound!

Mom pushed the bow back.

"*I* want to try," I said. "Just me."

"All right." Mom set the bow in place. "Go ahead."

I pulled the bow fast and made a scraping, growling noise like Dad's voice when he was sick. That was really better!

"Listen!" I said, and I put the bow at the starting place and made almost the same sound again. I did it over and over, pulling the bow faster and faster until it skidded away with a squeal like a yowling cat. "Lenny can't do that!"

Dad laughed, but Mom said, "Stop, Tessie. A violin is not a toy." She changed how I was holding the bow. "This time see how *gentle* you can be."

I tried my best, pulling the bow as lightly as I could. And for an instant, between a scratchy start and a scritchy end, the violin made a pretty sound.

"Oh!" I said, staring down the length of it. "Ooooh."

DAD GOT HIS camera and took pictures before we even ate breakfast. And a few days later, Mom showed me one of me. She got a pen and wrote something across the bottom.

"What are you writing?" I asked.

Mom answered, "'Tessie, three years old, with her first violin.'"

"Three-and-a-half," I said.

"Almost," she said, but she didn't change what she wrote.

"Can I have the picture?"

"Let's put it on the refrigerator," she said, and that's where it went.

C," I said. It was a Saturday afternoon, too cold to play outside, but Mom had made me an indoor game.

She nodded. "Very good. Now find me a B."

The white cards spread out on the table each showed a note on the five lines that meant music. Unsure, I picked one up.

"Close, but that's an A," my mother said. "Remember? A is in a space, and B is on that middle line right above it."

I frowned, wishing it wasn't so hard. And then one right after another, I spotted two cards with the B note. "B, B," I said. "B, B, B. Now can we make cookies?"

"I promised, didn't I? But while I get out the baking things, you might try to find that B on your violin."

"I can," I told her. "Do you think I can?"

Mom said, "I think you're the smartest going-on-four-year-old girl in the world, and if you want to play a B note, you will."

Dad came into the room, pulling on his jacket. He said, "And I think this little girl can do anything else she sets her mind to, too."

"Do you really have to go to the clinic?" Mom asked him. "It's Saturday, and you spent the morning there."

"I'll make it fast—just check on a coyote pup that Fish and Wildlife brought in yesterday. Want to go with me, Tessie? It's a cute little guy with fuzzy ears and big amber eyes."

I looked at my mother.

She said, "Only cookie bakers get to sample cookie dough. Stephen, really, Tessie has things she wants to do here."

"Tessie?" he asked.

"Can I see the pup tomorrow?"

"Sure." He sounded cheerful, but he looked disappointed.

"I'd like to see it," I told him.

"I know, squirt. Now make those cookies good, because I'm going to eat a dozen of them when I come home."

Later, once the cookies were cooling on a rack, Mom sat down at the piano and I went back to my violin. Over and over, I practiced a scale that began with deep notes played on the bottom string and climbed all the way to high notes played way over on the other side. My mom had taught me how.

I watched my fingers as I tried to match my violin's sounds to the piano's. My fingers didn't always land right the first time, but I never, ever, failed to wiggle them into place.

"You've got a good ear, Tessie," Mom said. "You got it from me."

Mostly I just went up the scale and back down, but sometimes I said, "Wait!" And then I worked on just one note, playing it until I heard a sound that made me happy.

On another day, summer now, I sat at a newspaper-covered table making a picture with finger paints. I painted blue sky and tried to understand what my parents were talking about in the next room.

Dad kept saying, "Don't rush things."

"I'm not," Mom answered. "But it's wrong to hold Tessie back, and I can't teach her much more. Already she's figuring out things that are beyond me."

"But formal lessons at four!"

"Richard Dreyden won't push her. Why, he won't even take her on unless she can show him she's ready."

"So you've already talked to Drey?"

"He's our friend, Stephen. I ran into him at the farmers market and he asked how she was doing. I wouldn't have brought it up otherwise."

"Yes, you would have."

I jabbed a finger into green paint and began drawing a tree. Green was my favorite color. I liked blue next best. My new favorite animal was a wildcat kitten that Dad was caring for at his clinic, but it probably would go back to the woods soon.

Favorites were important to know because grown-ups were always asking about them. They laughed if you didn't have an answer. Sometimes they laughed anyway and didn't tell you why your answer was funny.

I dotted red apples on the tree and tried to remember if I knew Mr. Dreyden. I didn't think so.

My father was still talking about him. He said, "I suppose it can't hurt to get Drey's opinion. But Sharon, if he says she's *not* ready, then that's that for now. Agreed?"

"Agreed. But he won't."

When my mother and I got to Mr. Dreyden's, he was working with a pupil in his studio at the back of his house. "They'll be finished soon," Mrs. Dreyden said, waving toward kitchen chairs. "You can keep me company while you wait."

While she and my mom talked, I edged close to the studio door, trying to make out what the voices inside were saying. I wished my mom had told me what went on in a real music lesson. How would Mr. Dreyden decide if I was ready?

Then Mrs. Dreyden said to me, "I hear you're getting pretty good on your violin. Is that true?"

"I don't know," I told her. "I just like it."

The voices in the studio stopped, and someone began playing violin music. I thought it sounded beautiful. Not perfect, exactly, like music on a CD, but beautiful, and it was *there,* just beyond a door. "*That's* how I want to play," I said.

"Then you'll have to work at it," Mrs. Dreyden told me. "That's one of my husband's best students."

When Mom and Mrs. Dreyden stopped looking at me, I very quietly opened the heavy door.

The studio was full of sunlight and music.

"So, Tessie, you want to be a violinist?" Mr. Dreyden said.

"Yes, please," I answered, taking my violin case from my mother and setting it on a sofa. I started to open it, but Mr. Dreyden waved a large hand. "Let's wait on that," he said. "First, I've got some games you might like." His big head and great, round shoulders made me think of a bear.

"What games?" I asked.

"Do you know how to play follow-the-leader?"

I nodded.

"Good! Then we'll start with that. I'll do something, and then you must try to do exactly the same thing." Mr. Dreyden clapped his hands together once, sharply. "Can you do that?"

I clapped the same way.

He clapped three times, and I did, also.

"How about this rhythm?" He clapped five times and gave the claps a beat. *Clap, clap, clap-clap, clap.* I gave him the rhythm right back.

"Not bad," he said. Then, grinning to show that he was going to tease me, he clapped out a much harder and much, much longer one.

I grinned back, because he couldn't trick me. I repeated it exactly, clap, for clap, for clap.

"Well!" Mr. Dreyden said, raising his eyebrows. "Pretty nice. Are your feet as smart as your hands?" He went over to the piano. "I'm going to play something, and I want you to skip or march or do whatever the music makes you feel like doing."

"Should I dance?"

"If you want."

But I thought dancing might seem babyish, so I skipped and walked in time to the beat.

Mr. Dreyden finished with loud, cheerful sounds. "Can you sing, too? How about singing this?" His deep voice traveled up and down a five-step ladder as he sang, *"Jaybird in a tree, fussing down at me."*

I sang it back to him in my high voice.

"Right on pitch," he said. Then he took one of my hands and studied it, rubbing his thumb on my palm and curling and straightening my fingers. "Well," he said, "maybe now's the time to get out our violins."

I took mine from its case, but when I held it out to my mother, Mr. Dreyden took it instead. "I'll tune for you today, but after this you must do it yourself." He plucked the strings, turned a peg, and plucked some more before handing my violin back. "There," he said. "Now let's play follow-the-leader."

Mr. Dreyden's violin looked like mine except it was larger and had a longer bow, and also it was a lighter

color, more yellow. He played a note on it, and I followed. Several notes and I matched those. Something
longer, like a song, and after two wrong starts, I played it,
too. And then, even though he didn't ask me to, I played
the best music I knew, which was some I'd made up from
all my favorite sounds.

After I was done, Mr. Dreyden didn't say anything for
a long time. Then he told me, "Miss Tess, if you would
like violin lessons, I would be happy to teach you."

I asked, "Why did you call me Miss Tess?"

"Because you look so serious. And because you've got
a start on some pretty grown-up talent."

WHEN MOM TOOK me for my weekly lessons, Mr. Dreyden would be waiting with a game or an idea for something fun. And pretty soon he gave me my own book of
short songs, and we always began a new one the same
way. He'd reach for his violin, and I'd cry, "No! Let me!"

I'd figure out the new music by reading the notes and
tapping time with my right foot. Mostly they were songs
I knew anyway, like "Twinkle, Twinkle, Little Star." No
matter how easy, though, when I played to the end of a
new one, Mr. Dreyden clasped his hands above his head
and cried, "Bravo! *Bravissimo!*"

Then one day he put a different book in front of me.
"The melody line from a Strauss waltz," he said. "Think
you can do it?"

"Yes!"

But I didn't know about waltzes, and after several tries I put my violin down. "There's something wrong with this music," I said.

Mr. Dreyden shook his head. "What's wrong is that in your head you're trying to march instead of dance."

"No, I'm not. I'm trying to play."

Mom said, "Tessie, don't be silly. You know that a three-four time signature means you give a quarter note one beat and you count three beats to a measure. I've explained and—"

Mr. Dreyden interrupted. "Why don't we show Tess?" He put on a CD. "Now *this* is a waltz!"

In time to the music, he took a step with one foot, brought his other foot next to it, and then stepped in place. Then he repeated the steps, only moving to the other side. "*One,* two, three," he counted. He reminded me of a dancing bear in a picture book. "*One,* two, three. *One,* two, three."

He bellowed, "Christine!" and when Mrs. Dreyden opened the studio door he said, "Come dance this with me!" He told Mom, "Mrs. Thaler, you dance with Tess."

Soon we were all dancing around the studio, circling the piano and squeezing between the sofa and a table. "*One,* two, three. *One,* two, three..."

After that, I didn't have any trouble playing waltzes.

WITH MR. DREYDEN teaching me, I quickly got into harder music, where I had to do more than just watch the notes and count. Before I was out of kindergarten, I'd learned to check key signatures for flats and sharps, so that I'd play the notes right the first time.

I started paying attention to the lines that Mr. Dreyden called *dynamics*. The long, widening wedges that meant *get louder,* and the wedges going in the other direction that meant *softer now, go softer* were like one of his games. Sometimes I tried to make a sound fade away so slowly that even Mr. Dreyden couldn't hear exactly when it disappeared.

And even though I couldn't read all the words printed on my music, I learned to press down on my bow when Mr. Dreyden said *forte!* I played as quietly as I could when he whispered *pianissimo;* I plucked my violin's strings when he said *pizzicato;* and at *cantabile* I tried to make my violin sing.

If I wasn't sure I was doing something right, I'd look to see if the wrinkles on Mr. Dreyden's forehead were little or deep. Sometimes I'd find him watching me with a look like he had just received a wonderful, unexpected present.

Just before my sixth birthday, Mom came home with a CD she'd bought. "Tessie, I've a treat for you," she said. "It's a Mozart symphony."

At first I only half listened because I was busy putting together a puzzle. But then the sounds filled my head, crowding out the puzzle pieces, and I went to sit close to the music pouring out of the player.

I shut my eyes and imagined that it was flying up into the air and filling the sky with beautiful colors. When the music ended I started it over again, and this time I saw shapes of sound running across staffs of music; saw more notes played more ways than I had words for.

I ran for paper and crayons, and I covered page after page with notes and lines and swirls, using every crayon I had because there were so many kinds of sounds.

Mom looked over my shoulder. "Whatever are you doing?"

"Drawing the symphony," I said, "so that I can play it. Listen."

I got my violin and found the first note, which I'd colored pale purple because it was a halting note, a note feeling its way. Then I played all my pages straight through. I played exciting runs and quiet, slow sections; played steep climbs and sad little falls, although, of course, I couldn't make my violin sound like all the different instruments. It just sounded like itself.

I played after I ran out of pages and kept playing until I lost my way. "I can't remember what's next," I said. "I need to hear it again."

"Tessie, when did you learn that?" Mom asked in an odd voice.

"Just now," I answered. "It's what you put on for me to listen to."

"But you must have known it from someplace!"

I shook my head. I knew I'd never heard that perfect music before because if I had, I wouldn't have forgotten it.

MOM TOOK MY drawings to my violin lesson the next day. After I'd played them for Mr. Dreyden, he looked at me with an expression as odd as the tone in Mom's voice the afternoon before. "Good lord," he said. "I never dreamed...Oh, my dear young Tess."

Mom and Dad talked late that night, their muffled words going on long after they put me to bed.

At breakfast the next morning the conversation became a triangle. Mom talked to me. "Tessie, your father is having a hard time grasping the significance of what you've done."

Dad talked to her. "Sharon, I'm not minimizing Tessie's accomplishment."

Mom told me, "We've been discussing the next step. I think it's time to place you with a teacher who can make the most of your talent. But your father doesn't understand—"

Dad interrupted her with a wave. "I'm not saying she doesn't have a gift, but we've got Drey to thank for bringing it out. He's a fine musician and a good friend, and I don't see how you can tell him we want somebody better."

"You'd put a friend before your daughter?" Mom asked. She turned back to me. "Tessie, get your violin and play the start of that symphony for your father."

"I heard it last night," Dad told her.

"Tessie," Mom said, "your violin."

Dad folded his arms across his chest and kept them that way while I played. He stopped looking so certain, though.

When I lowered my violin, Mom asked, "Well, Stephen? Do you really think Drey's feelings are more important than Tessie's future?"

Dad put his hand under my chin and tilted my face so that he could look into my eyes. "Pumpkin?"

Because I wasn't sure what he was asking, I didn't answer.

Mom said, "Remember I was right about when to give Tessie a violin and when to start her on lessons."

Dad smoothed back my hair before he stood up. "I hope you *were* right. I wish I could be as sure as you." He pulled on his jacket. "Do as you think necessary, but don't lost sight of our daughter. She's still a child."

After he left, Mom loaded dishes into the dishwasher while I stayed at the table and thought over everything they'd said. When I was sure I had it right, I said, "Please don't make Mr. Dreyden stop being my teacher."

Mom didn't answer, so I said it again louder. "Mom, please don't make Mr. Dreyden stop being my teacher."

She wedged a pitcher into the bottom rack and then sat down next to me. "Your father trusts me to know what's best for you, Tessie, and you must also." She gave me a smile that I didn't all-the-way believe. "It's not as if you won't ever see Mr. Dreyden again. You can visit him, and when you give your first recital, we'll be sure to send him an invitation."

# TESS

Meg takes Amy to a 4-H meeting after supper.
Then Dad gets called back to his veterinary clinic and I go along, staying in the reception room while he and the nighttime assistant work on a Lab pup that tangled with a raccoon. Like our house, the clinic is a mix of familiar and new. Same animal scale, new vinyl floor. Same molded plastic chairs, new dog biscuit jars on the counter.

While I wait, I look at Dad's bulletin board, which I remember because I used to take care of it. Sandwiched among pet photos are pictures of some of the wild creatures that my father helps rehabilitators care for. There's one spectacular shot of a great horned owl, and when Dad's assistant, Janie, comes out to get something, I ask her about it.

"That's Midnight," she says. "A bow hunter wounded him last fall, and the poor owl was here so long he and your father become friends."

"Is Dad doing very much rehab work?" I ask.

"As much as he can," Janie tells me. "It's where his heart is." She looks at me with an expression I can't read. "Too bad that kind of work doesn't pay the bills."

"HOW'S THE DOG?" I ask Dad as we pull out of the parking lot.

"Full of stitches, but he'll live to get into more mischief. The last time we saw that pup, he'd tried to hassle a skunk!"

"I heard about Midnight," I say. "Were you able to fix him up?"

"That tough old guy?" Dad chuckles. "I took Amy to watch his release just last month. It was the funniest thing. Midnight flapped to a nearby tree and then gave us a long, knowing look before he flew off, strong as ever. He almost seemed to be saying good-bye."

"Or maybe thanks," I suggest.

"That might be a stretch," Dad replies, but I can tell he's tickled.

"So," I say, "does Amy hang around the clinic much?"

"All she can. Just the way you used to."

He chuckles again, and I know we're both remembering how seriously I took my Saturday-morning job washing kennel runs. Dad used to say the president of the United States himself probably couldn't hire better help. Feeling very worldly, I'd say, "But we better hope he does."

Now I ask, "And is Amy as good a worker as I was?"

"Not quite as stick-to-a-task reliable with cleanup chores, but she's got a feel for the animals. She knocks herself out caring for the boarding pets, and I've seen her sit for hours soothing a cat that's come through a hard time."

"You think she'll become a vet?"

"She's got a lot of years to decide that, but it wouldn't surprise me. Vet or wildlife biologist maybe. You should have seen her with Midnight. She'd stand at his cage and talk to him, and he'd stare back as though he understood every word. I'm sure his good-bye was for both of us."

I'm not jealous, but I do feel a little forgotten hearing how Amy's taken over my old job and turned it into more than I ever made of it. Maybe if things had been different—maybe if I'd never started playing violin or maybe if I'd started later, hadn't had the talent, hadn't left Montana—I'd be the one still helping Dad.

As though he's been following my thoughts, Dad says, "There was once a time I thought you might choose some kind of an outdoors career yourself, but then nothing seemed to have the pull on you that your violin did."

"No," I say.

We drive several blocks before Dad asks, "Are you going to tell me what went wrong?"

"I don't know myself, exactly," I answer. I hesitate and then ask, "Dad, would you mind if I stayed here? Permanently, I mean, and not go back to New York?"

"This is your home," he says, "and you know I'd love to have you back here. But that would be a pretty major U-turn for you. You want to talk to your old man about it?"

I shake my head. "It's something I've got to figure out for myself."

He nods. "Well, when you do want to talk, remember I'm ready to listen. I may not be able to help, but I'll try my hardest and—"

"I know, Dad. And that's all a mule can do, right?"

He laughs. "I haven't heard that in years."

"You're the one who used to say it. Remember? When I'd get mad because I couldn't do something just right, you'd tell me, 'Do your best, Tess. That's all a mule can do'..." My voice trails off as I think about that. "Sometimes that's not enough, is it?"

"No," he says, and the way he says that one word, I know he's aching for me. "Sometimes it's not."

The house is quiet now, but the light of a full moon keeps me awake. My mind turns like the second hand on a clock sweeping past each mark—Dad, Mom, my violin, Mr. Dreyden, Ben, New York, Montana, Meg, Amy, Midnight, Katharina, her father's old violin. . . .

Poor Katharina, thinking that after all these years it could just be taken out and played.

Violins shouldn't disappoint. There ought to be a law against it.

The moonlight is bright enough that I can see the shelf of dolls that someone's moved from my old room to here. They're old friends: Mama Bunny and Ellie Elephant, the brocade Dancing Lady, and Miss Petunia. They're in the wrong order, though, and wearing one another's clothes. Amy's doing, I guess.

I get up to wind the Dancing Lady on her music box stand, and then I switch on the ancient melody that lulled me to sleep when I was a little girl.

I wonder what I could tell Ben if I called him, if I knew where to call. He'd want to know when I'm returning to New York. I wouldn't know what to answer.

SOMETIME LATER I'm jolted awake by a nightmare in which my hands are tightly bound and their backs laced with sutures. Someone is taking away my violin, saying, "You won't need this anymore. You won't need this anymore." My palms hurt from my fingernails digging into them.

*Katharina,* I think, as I shake off the bad dream. Seeing her scars must have planted the seed for the nightmare.

I get up and rub lotion on my hands, and before I go back to bed I open my window to the reassuring *spit-spit-spit* of a lawn sprinkler. It's one sound I never hear in New York.

I WAKE BEFORE seven o'clock the next morning, dress, and take my extra camping clothes down to the basement where Dad and Meg are loading gear into backpacks. They've got stuff spread out from one side of the playroom to the other.

Dad asks, "Think it'll all go in?"

"I don't know," I answer, eyeing how much is left: sleeping bags and ground pads, cooking utensils, rainwear, hats and gloves for early mornings and cool evenings, a water filter, a collapsible stove and fuel, matches, cups, powdered milk, freeze-dried food. "I guess it's got to."

I offer to get breakfast for everyone, and Meg's "Thanks" sounds really grateful.

Amy doesn't help so much as bounce around, but her enthusiasm is catching and I find myself beginning to look forward to the day. Or maybe I'm just excited because I can still lift my pack once it's bulging with my share of the supplies.

From home, it's a short walk to the trailhead, but it feels like moving from one world to another. One moment we're striding along Rattlesnake Drive, keeping out of the way of cars, our talk drowned out by the power mowers of a lawn-care crew. Minutes later we're in a cool, quiet forest world where insects clack, conifers scent the air, and the ground feels good underfoot.

We stop near a Forest Service bulletin board to adjust our packs, and Amy wants to know about a pair of notices that show a bear and a lunging cougar. Although she stands on tiptoe, they're too high up for her to read.

I tell her that they say not to wear purple in the backcountry unless you want to be mistaken for a huckleberry.

"No! Really?"

I scan the papers. "They warn against surprising animals on the trail or leaving out food where it will attract them."

"Everybody knows not to do that," she says.

A half mile in along Rattlesnake Creek, we get to Spring Gulch and the Stuart Peak trail. Reaching the top is our day's goal: 7,960 feet high. About eight miles according to the trail sign—and all of it uphill—and in my opinion the sooner we start, the more likely it is we'll make it.

But Meg wants to detour to inspect the remains of an old bridge. "It's part of the Rattlesnake's history. Come on. You all should see it."

She veers down a narrow path, the rest of us following, and then disappears into a thicket of shrubs. Amy and I start after her, but Dad puts a hand on my shoulder and points. Amy stops, also.

At first I don't see anything special, but then I hear something fly close by my ear.

*There it is.* An iridescent green hummingbird no bigger than my thumb hovers in midair. I flash Dad a grin, thinking that the bird is what he wanted me to see, but he shakes his head and points again. "Look in the bush behind her."

Sitting side by side on a thin branch are two baby hummers. They can't be much more than an inch long each, and while I watch, the hovering mother bird pokes her needle-like beak into a baby's mouth.

"She's feeding it!" Amy exclaims, and immediately the parent hummer speeds by us, out of sight.

"You scared her," I say.

"I didn't!"

Dad motions us to be quiet. The mother bird has returned and is now gathering nectar from a small cascade
of white blossoms, the only ones left on a shrub almost
done with blooming.

We watch her go back and forth between flowers and
the babies, getting food and feeding them. The birds are
so tiny, it's like watching creatures in a fairy world.

And then, suddenly, this other hummingbird, rusty
orange and half again the size of the green one, swoops
in like a dive-bomber taking over. It samples the flowers
and then flits furiously back and forth and around,
wings buzzing with a metallic *whirrrr,* and there is no
way the tiny green bird is going to get more food for her
babies.

When I look to see how the babies are doing, they've
disappeared. Then the adults are gone, too.

"Wow," Dad says. "In all my years of birding, I've
never seen a hummingbird feed its young."

"I hate that big one," Amy says. "Don't you, Tess?"

"Well, not hate it, but I feel sorry for the littler ones
that got driven away. They were calliopes, right, Dad?"

He nods, looking delighted that I've remembered
their name. "*Stellula calliope,* and the aggressive one was
a rufous."

I'd like to wait and see if either comes back, but Meg
calls, "Are you three lost?"

"Coming," Dad answers, and he leads the way through
a final stretch of thick bushes.

Amy, treading almost on my heels, turns the Latin into rap. *"Stel-luuu-la-ca-li-o-pe, Stel-looo-loo . . ."*

WE EMERGE AT the top of an old concrete bridge abutment. Another crumbling support stands opposite, and the creek rushes below, no longer spanned.

"What is this place?" I ask, watching Meg work her way down the bank.

Dad answers, "The original way into the upper Rattlesnake, from back when there were still people living up here. Right, Meg?"

"You got it," she agrees, halting on a rocky crescent of shore. "From where you are, one road went up to the Spring Gulch meadow and another followed the main creek. Every time homesteaders like Frederik Bottner and his family wanted to visit town, they had to cross this bridge."

I look back at the thicket we've just come through. It's hard to imagine that anything as solid as a road could have disappeared so completely.

"Who's Frederik Bottner?" Amy asks, but before Meg can answer, Amy starts peppering Dad with other questions. "Do hummingbirds have just two babies? What do their nests look like? Do you think the babies went back there after that big hummer scared them away? What's his name again?"

"It was a rufous."

Meg wets the tip of a finger and runs it over a bit of the bridge remains. "The concrete's holding up. Of course, this bridge was built to handle everything from farm wagons to logging trucks."

As we backtrack to the Stuart Peak trail, Amy is still talking about the hummingbirds. "I wish Midnight would come scare the rufous. That would serve it right."

She reminds me of a hummingbird herself, the way she's tiny and quick, darting off to check things that catch her eye and then returning to hover by Dad's side.

"Except I don't want Midnight to *eat* the rufous," she says. "Owls don't eat other birds, do they? Pop, where do you think Midnight is now? Do owls have a big range? Because if they do..."

Meg, bringing up the rear with me, says, "Your father has got the patience of Job."

Meg's still in historian mode as we start up Spring Gulch. She tells me that a schoolhouse once stood in the vacant meadow off to our right. "Just a one-room grade school with a couple of outhouses in the back."

As the gulch narrows, the meadow gives way to a lush, thick tangle of leafy shrubs and undergrowth. Dad's striding out in front in his easygoing, hike-all-day pace that I remember. When I was little, he'd usually slow it down so I could keep up, but sometimes he'd forget and then I'd have to run a couple of steps for every few I walked. Now it's Amy who's doing the walk-run, and the two of them are talking as fast as her feet are going.

"Amy sure is a happy kid," I comment.

"Mostly," Meg replies. "We've moved around a lot and she hasn't always had the easiest time fitting in to new places, but this past year's she's really blossomed and developed some confidence. That's largely your dad's doing, of course." Meg smiles ruefully. "Though sometimes she's a little too confident for her own good."

Meg waves toward a distant pair of bushy trees that tower maybe a hundred feet tall. "What do you want to bet there used to be a house there?" she says.

"How can you tell?" I ask.

"Those Lombardy poplars are a sure giveaway. They're not native to this area, so somebody planted them, probably as a shelter from wind. And now, although the people are gone, the trees show where they once lived."

"Cool," I say, impressed even if the explanation is obvious now that I've heard it. And when I spot three scraggly apple trees a ways farther on, I say, "And those must have been planted, too, right?"

"Right you are," Meg says. "Somebody's orchard Lombardy poplars, lilacs, apple trees—none is native to Montana, so when you see them growing in what seems like a wilderness, you know it hasn't always been completely wild."

By now, Amy's back to rapping Latin, and she's got Dad doing it with her. Apparently the full name of the rust-orange hummer was *Stelasphorus rufus.* Stel-*as*-phor-*us*-ru-*fus, Stel*-luuu-*la-ca*-li-*o*-pe.

Meg asks me, "How much more Latin do you think your dad knows?"

"I don't know," I answer, "but I saw him put his bird book in his pack."

She shows me one more remnant of the valley's history, a caved-in section of bank that she says is the remains of an exploratory mining pit. "Back when gold and silver were coming out of places not fifty miles away, prospectors had high hopes all over this area."

"Did they ever find anything?" I ask.

"Not around here, although I know of at least one small mine that was worked off and on for years, and I imagine there were others."

The trail makes a hairpin turn around the head of Spring Gulch, and with that we start really climbing. The valley bottom drops rapidly behind us, a spreading panorama of many shades of green, and my legs and lungs start to feel the strain of the long ascent. When, finally, Dad announces, "Lunchtime," I'm the first to hit the ground.

WE EAT SPRAWLED against our backpacks, on a slope where huckleberry bushes thick with the beginnings of berries grow in open shade. Dad says we should remember the spot and come back when it's time for picking.

Meg says, "I think I'll take a little walk," and disappears around a bend in the trail.

"She has to use the bathroom," Amy tells me.

"I figured."

"So when we get home, will you teach me to play your violin?" she asks.

"What made you think of that?"

"Nothing. Will you?"

"We'll see," I say. I lean back and close my eyes.

A minute later I'm startled upright by a loud squeal. Amy is grinning at me from behind her cupped hands, and a blade of grass is stretched taut between her pressed-together thumbs. She says, "Say you'll teach me your violin!"

"I said, we'll see."

"If you don't, I'll make you sorry!" She blows the grass blade right in my ear. I push her away and we end up rolling into Dad, who groans.

"So," Amy says to me, "how long will it take me to get good?"

"At what?"

"Your violin! When you teach me!"

"That's *if* I teach you," I say. "And it would depend on what you mean by 'good.' But a long time, anyway."

"How long?"

"I don't know."

"How long did it take you?"

"I don't know," I repeat. "There's still an awful lot I haven't learned but...Good enough so somebody would want to hear me play? I guess half a dozen years. That's about how long it took before I played my first recital."

"Six *years*?" Amy says. "My best friend at school only

started piano last fall, and she's already played in two recitals."

Meg, returning in time to hear Amy, says, "Those were different from the kind of recital Tess is talking about." She looks at the uphill trail in front of us, sighs, and asks, "Well, shall we do it?"

# TESSIE

Like a general pushing her army, Mom marched me through one, two, three violin teachers before she came to Mr. Capianelli, who told her that only rarely had he had the honor of teaching a pupil with my gifts.

I was nine, beginning fourth grade, and playing a bigger violin now.

Mr. Capianelli was new to Montana, having come to Missoula for a year's sabbatical from his professional obligations. He hadn't planned to take on students but made an exception for me.

At the start of each lesson, while I tuned and warmed up, Mr. Capianelli talked to Mom about all the great musicians he knew, including some violinists he'd taught.

What I liked best about Mr. Capianelli was that when I played my violin, he played his, and he played so, so well. He would lead, and I'd try to match him, and when I was able to, I could hardly hold my excitement inside.

I didn't like it, though, when he explained what I needed to work on, because he explained it to Mom instead of to me. "Her fourth finger needs strengthening," he'd say, marking passages in my exercise book. "Please see that Tess spends extra time with these."

I spent a lot of time practicing. Dad left for his clinic really early in the morning, and my first practice session of the day was the hour before the school bus. Then when I came home from school, Mom worked with me until she needed to start dinner. She called it directed practice because she told me what to do from what Mr. Capianelli had told her.

After dinner I played for another hour, and that was when I got to play whatever I wanted. If Dad was home he'd listen and smile and sometimes he'd tease me. He'd say he'd heard a violin could make a sound that would crack glass and why hadn't I learned to do that?

Sometimes Mom and Dad argued about how much I practiced. "It's not natural," Dad said. "She ought to be doing more of the things other kids do. Soccer or Girl Scouts. 4-H, maybe."

"Tessie isn't like other kids," Mom answered.

They compromised. Mom ruled six days, but Saturdays belonged to Dad and me. I began going with him to the clinic on Saturday mornings. His assistant let me help feed some of the animals, and arranging pet photos on the lobby bulletin board became my special job.

On Saturday afternoons Dad and I would do whatever I chose. He would ask if I wanted to invite a friend
over to play or to go to the movies with us, but I'd say no.
Instead I'd ask him to take me exploring. We went all
over, along canyon creeks in the Bitterroots and across
the hillsides west of town, but mostly we hiked in the
Rattlesnake woods, near home.

With a flourish, Mr. Capianelli placed new music before me. "Brahms's Sonata no. 1 in G Major," he said. "Our work from now on, because with this you will make your debut."

He turned to my mother. "I think that by late spring, Tess will be ready to give her first recital."

"I've been in recitals before," I told him. "My last teacher—"

"No, no!" Mr. Capianelli exclaimed as though I'd said something amusing. "I don't mean to hide you among a dozen children in a program that only parents could enjoy. No! You, my precocious Tess, will give your own performance, and I promise that it will be one no one ever forgets!"

I held back a giggle. That was just the way Mr. Capianelli talked, and I'd learned to listen for the sense beneath his words. Besides, the music he'd set out was pages longer than anything I'd ever tried. *Of course, I'll need my own recital,* I thought. *There won't be time left for anybody else if I play all this.*

My lessons increased from one to two a week, and Mom began driving me to school and picking me up afterward so that I didn't waste practice time sitting on a school bus. And we had to squeeze in other sessions, too, when I could work with the pianist Mom hired to accompany me.

That part was mostly fun, but one time I asked Mom, "Can I skip today? I'm tired."

"I don't see how you can," she said. But then she put her arm around me. "I know how hard you're working. What if you do just one hour right now, and then afterward we'll go to that new ice cream place and you can order whatever you want. And I won't even tell you not to spoil your dinner!"

Mom rarely mentioned the recital around Dad, and I didn't think he realized how special it was going to be. Not until Mom brought home the invitations she'd had made up. They weren't just copies of something she'd put together on her computer, but real ones like for weddings.

---

YOU ARE CORDIALLY INVITED TO A VIOLIN RECITAL
GIVEN BY TESS THALER,
NINE-YEAR-OLD STUDENT OF MR. VINCENT CAPIANELLI,
WITH MRS. BESS ARMITAGE AT THE PIANO.
SUNDAY, APRIL 28, AT THREE O'CLOCK
MUSIC RECITAL HALL, UNIVERSITY OF MONTANA

---

Dad exploded. His face reddened, and a vein in his neck pulsed in and out. "What do you think you are doing with this child? Do you have any idea?..." He got louder and louder, although I'd never, ever heard Dad yell before.

I covered my ears and slipped away to my bedroom, but my parents' angry voices followed and pushed through my hands.

"Mr. Capianelli believes..."

"...exploiting her... Who the hell does he think he is?"

"Good experience working with an accompanist..."

"...and a recital hall! What is this going to cost?"

"...just renting..."

"You're out of your mind," Dad said. "A pianist, formal invitations... She's a nine-year-old, for god's sake. You have gone way over the top."

I took my blanket into my closet and shut the door. Curled up in the dark, I closed out everything but the music that I carried in my head.

I wore a white organdy dress, white shoes, and thin, high white socks. Mom tied and retied a blue ribbon that held my hair out of my eyes, and she dabbed a bit of pale pink gloss on my lips. Dad rubbed it off with a handkerchief. "Do you want me to leave right now and take Tess with me?"

I tugged on his hand. "Please stop being mad. I'm going to play really good."

We were getting ready in a classroom a few doors down from the auditorium where I'd perform. People passed by, looked in, and waved.

Mom waved back. "Oh," she said, "the Smith-Callahans have come," and "Dear Mrs. Breyley is here with her cronies."

When she took me down the hall to use the women's room a last time, we found it full of more ladies that Mom knew, and they all told me how sweet I looked.

Then the bathroom emptied, and then the corridor, and Mom said, "Three o'clock!"

She led me around a back way into the recital hall, into a space hidden from the audience. Out on the brightly lit stage, Mrs. Armitage already sat at the grand piano. Mr. Capianelli strode out and introduced himself and then began talking about me and the music I was going to present.

Mom straightened my dress and said, "Play your best. Don't forget to smile." She gave me a little push when Mr. Capianelli gestured for me to join him. "I'm counting on you."

People applauded, and then Mr. Capianelli left the stage. I raised my violin and nodded to Mrs. Armitage to begin, just the way we'd practiced.

I played with my eyes mostly closed, because that was how I listened best. Sometimes, though, I watched my fingers flying through especially hard parts. Once I glimpsed pleased faces and understood that the audience liked my music. I felt glad, because I liked it, too.

Actually, I *loved* it. This was the most gorgeous, shining violin music I knew, and I played every note the very best I could. The lovely sounds carried me along and made me forget everything else. Except that there was a moment in a pause between two sections when I glimpsed the audience again. For an instant it was as if I could see what they were seeing: me in my white dress, so carefully positioning my bow for the next downstroke.

And then it was time to play again, and I closed my eyes.

When I was finished—after the final notes faded away—everything was silent for a moment. Then people began clapping, and the clapping grew louder. A camera flashed, and Mom put a big bouquet of pink roses in my arms. With my violin they made a lot to hold on to, but I held them close and smelled how sweet they were.

Then we went out to the front lobby, where everybody was sipping fruit punch and nibbling on little cookies. They lined up to tell my parents and Mr. Capianelli and me what a pleasure my performance had been. Mr. Dreyden, my very first violin teacher, gave me a big hug. "You played beautifully," he said.

I asked why his eyes were shiny. "Are they?" he asked. "Must be hay fever."

Even after we went out to the parking lot, people kept saying nice things. One man called me a "dear little wunderkind" and said he'd like to hear just one more piece. I thought he was asking me to play again, but Mom covered my hands with hers and shook her head. If she hadn't, I might have taken out my violin and played a whole second recital, I was that wound up.

"WHAT DOES *wunderkind* mean?" I asked.

"It means you did yourself proud," Dad answered, his eyes meeting mine in the rearview mirror.

"It's a German word," Mom told me. "It means 'wonder child.' That's you, Tessie. Our wonder child."

"How about stopping for an ice cream cone?" Dad asked. "I'll treat to two toppings."

"Not in her good dress," Mom answered.

Anyway, I wasn't hungry even for ice cream. My stomach still twirled with excitement, and I felt like I did after a whole day of going on rides at the county fair: tired but full of happiness.

That night, when Mom and Dad came in to turn my light out, I asked, "What was that word again? The one about how wonderful I was?"

Dad frowned. "Tessie, you mustn't—" he began, but Mom cut him off.

"Wunderkind," she said. "You're our darling little wunderkind who amazes everyone."

*Wunderkind.* I went to sleep trying on the word, and the next morning, I learned another word that meant almost the same thing. I found it in a newspaper that had been put at my place at the breakfast table. It was opened up to a photo showing people clapping and me hanging on to my violin and the roses. Mom read the caption with me: "Child prodigy Tess Thaler, nine, delights an audience with her grown-up skills."

Wunderkind. Prodigy. Me.

# FREDERIK
## 1905–1906

Frederik Bottner awakened in the half-light before dawn, jostled by the sleeping stirrings of the stranger who shared his train seat. He glanced at the dim landscape passing by the window and then looked harder, trying to make out if a silvery gleam high on the hillsides might be snow.

*Surely not, not in September.* But then, Frederik had no references for deciphering country like this.

Through a fitful night, he had been aware in snatches of the train passing from short-grass prairie into Montana's western mountains. Its coal-fed engine had labored up inclines, jerking him awake over and over as it pulled passenger coaches and boxcars over high trestles and through dark tunnels.

Boxcars: They were emigrant cars; each rented by a homesteading family for $22.50 and filled with chests and plow blades, seed bags and rootstock all rubbing and

creaking together; each packed with nervous animals un-
steady on rumbling floors.

Frederik's horse, Patch, was in one of them, along
with the few head of livestock and some tools that were
about all Frederik still owned now that the South Dakota
homestead was sold and the debts on it cleared. His be-
longings didn't half fill the car, and he'd shared the rental
with a family who needed extra space.

*That* is *a dusting of snow,* he thought. *How early does
winter come to Montana, anyway?* There was so much
he didn't know about this place he'd decided on. But
at least the journey was over. The train slowed, whistle
blowing, as it pulled into Missoula. Outside the window,
railroad men shouted orders and did work that made
metal clang on metal.

Frederik got his traveling bundle and his father's violin from the overhead rack.


THE FIVE-MILE wagon journey from town to a crossing
over Rattlesnake Creek took Frederik and his Uncle Joe
until early afternoon, even without the livestock they'd
arranged to have brought after them.

"Are we about to your place?" Frederik asked, as his
uncle guided the team onto the narrow bridge.

"No! We've still got several miles to go. And more
getting to know each other to do, also. What I want you
to tell me—"

Whatever Uncle Joe's question was, it didn't get asked,

because just then a shot rang out, frightening the horses and throwing Joe into a struggle to keep the wagon on the bridge. Frederik, scrambling to the back where Patch was tethered, saw a young man gallop by on a large roan.

"*Mein*..." His uncle swore, half in German, half in English, as the wagon lurched back from a near plunge into the creek. Frederik grabbed for Patch's lead while his uncle fought to bring the careening team to a halt. And then, as the wagon pitched into the long ascent up from the bridge, the horses slowed of their own accord.

"Who was that?" Frederik asked when he returned to his seat.

"Augie O'Leary," Uncle Joe answered, sounding half strangled with anger. "Young hooligan."

"But what was he doing? Did he shoot at us?"

"More likely shot to scare. He and his father, Naill, do their best to sour this valley, and for no reason other than they're plain crazy mean. I was able to buy my place because of Augie. The Middlers, that I got it from, pulled out rather than let their daughter get tangled up with him."

"Oh!" Frederik considered the information about the O'Learys before turning his attention to the rest of what his uncle had said. "You're not homesteading?" Frederik asked. He wondered why anybody would want to pay for land when you could get it from the government for free.

"The Middlers wanted to sell, and four hundred fifty dollars for a quarter section and all the buildings—it was a bargain compared with working up a place from scratch."

"But you got the O'Learys for neighbors?"

"I keep a good fence between me and them," Uncle Joe said. "I stay clear of Naill's land and his mine claim, and I generally don't have trouble."

UNCLE JOE'S PLACE, one of the homes farthest out in the Rattlesnake, was reached by a wagon-track road that dipped and swayed alongside the main creek.

The ride took Frederik and his uncle past ever more isolated dwellings where men walked behind mule-pulled plows to turn over field stubble, children dug potatoes, and women stirred wash in open kettles. Small plots of cleared land hugged the creek bottom or canted upward onto brushy hillsides where cattle and sheep foraged among tree stumps.

His uncle, following Frederik's gaze, said, "A lot of this country was logged for railroad ties back in the eighties."

Finally they turned onto a pair of tracks that led through a ragged field to a small cabin.

"This is it," Joe said. "Lots to be done, and I'll be glad for your help."

Just then a voice shouted, "Bottner!" and they turned to see three people on horseback coming from the road.

As the riders neared, Frederik recognized the roan horse and realized one of the people was Augie O'Leary.

The others were a large, rough-looking man and a girl about Frederik's own age. They led packhorses loaded down with panniers, tools, and bedrolls.

Uncle Joe, flushing, muttered, "Dear Lord, I thought we made a bargain: I'd be civil to Naill O'Leary when I saw him, and You'd make sure I didn't see him."

The riders halted a few feet off, and the older man told Uncle Joe, "Augie said you was bringing new people. You warn 'em to stay off my land."

"Now, Naill," Frederik's uncle answered in a calm voice, "my nephew Frederik here is all the new people, and I'll see he knows what's yours. Nobody's looking to encroach."

Augie pulled up a deer rifle and casually aimed it just past Frederik. Grinning, he jerked it back in mock recoil.

Frederik and his uncle both started angrily forward but halted when Naill ordered his son, "Put it away."

The girl, looking annoyed and embarrassed, told Frederik, "Don't mind my brother. He doesn't have good sense or manners, either one."

She had green eyes and shining red hair, and when she smiled, Frederik saw dimples dent in at both sides of her mouth. "I'm Maureen O'Leary," she said, "and I'll like having a new neighbor. Will you be going into town to high school?"

"I don't know," Frederik answered, with no idea what the plans for him were.

"I'll be starting my freshman year after we come down from the mine," Maureen said. "Maybe we can ride in together some."

"He's too old for school," Naill O'Leary told her and ended the talk by wheeling his horse around. "You, too, if you get any ideas I don't like. Let's go."

After they'd left Frederik said, "I see what you mean about them souring things. Why were you even nice to that man?"

"It's just good business to get along with neighbors," Uncle Joe answered, pausing to tamp tobacco into his pipe. "Besides, I feel sorry for Naill O'Leary. Ever since his wife left him, he's poured his soul into a worthless mine. He's not the first person gone addled over losing a spouse."

*Like my father, though that was different,* Frederik thought, as Joe went on, "I've been told his wife ran off years ago, saying she was tired of living with a man who'd never make good."

"Maureen's mother, you mean?"

"Yes." Uncle Joe looked at Frederik sharply. "And Augie's."

"And the O'Learys were the reason the Middlers left? Frederik wanted to be sure he had it straight.

"That's so," Joe answered. Then he laughed and slapped Frederik on the shoulder. "Of course, the Middlers didn't have any son to notice a pretty girl with green eyes. If they had, that might have changed things."

Maureen O'Leary was on Frederik's mind when he awoke in the loft above the one room of Uncle Joe's log house. The March morning was still dark, but even earlier he'd heard Uncle Joe leave to go into the mountains to check his traplines, a two-day job that he did three times a week.

Now, with all the morning's chores to do alone, Frederik quickly arose and hurried to work. He chopped through creek ice to get water for the livestock. He tossed hay into feeders and fed grain to shoving, pregnant ewes. He split firewood, filled kerosene lamps, and shoveled the lane where new snowdrifts had blocked it.

He had to rush to be done in time to saddle Patch by six-thirty. Maureen would be coming by soon on her way into Missoula, and Frederik wanted to ride in with her.

In the half year since Frederik had come to Montana, he hadn't enrolled in high school. Snow and distance made a daily round-trip impossible, and Uncle Joe had looked relieved when Frederik said he guessed he'd be better helping here than spending five days a week in town.

Lately, though, he'd been riding in with Maureen on Sunday mornings and also returning to town some Friday afternoons to ride back with her. During the school week she stayed with an aunt.

Frederik had met the aunt. She was a cold-seeming woman who bossed Maureen around while saying she was only teaching what her sister—Maureen's mother—should have. She made attending Sunday Mass a condition of Maureen's staying with her.

Frederik cinched in his horse's belly strap. "Behave yourself, Patch," he said. "Holding your breath won't make me put this saddle away." He tightened the strap another notch. "And you know you like going out."

The brown-and-white paint horse just snorted.

ONCE ON THE ROAD, Frederik didn't have to wait long for Maureen. She brought her horse up next to his, and after exchanging greetings they rode quietly side by side.

Not that Frederik didn't have things he wanted to say. He just didn't know quite how.

Uncle Joe, when he'd realized how regularly Frederik was making these rides, had teased, "Nephew, fifteen's too young to be falling in love."

"I'm not," Frederik had answered, his face growing hot. "Keeping Maureen company is just something to do."

But now, as daylight came and they stopped to watch their warm breath turn into a vapor gauze over ice-crystaled pine boughs, Frederik thought how beautiful she made the winter mornings.

When Maureen showed him the branches of red twigs outlined by the blinding brightness of a climbing sun, Frederik noticed how the sunlight made a golden glow along the edge of her cheek.

"You're not listening to a word I'm saying," she accused.

"I am too."

And he was, if not to her words about what a pretty pattern the branches made, then to her voice, with all its lilting shades. *Like a violin,* he thought. *Like music.*

Now how he wished he could play the violin the way his father had, because he'd like to play it for Maureen. He'd like to make it say what he didn't have words for on this still winter morning.

Then the stillness was disturbed by snow shaking from treetops across the creek. There was a shouted order and the sound of movement in the forest.

Maureen's face turned anxious. "Let's hurry," she said. "That's probably Pa and Augie bringing down a sled of wood, and there's no point in them seeing you riding with me."

"Would they mind?" Frederik asked.

"They mind everything."

Frederik swung his pick and then shoveled out another few inches of irrigation ditch before pausing. The July day seemed as hot as the worst of winter had been cold. He wiped away some of the perspiration that streamed down his face and burned his eyes. *One more hard job.*

But Frederik had to admit that all the work was bringing results.

He and his uncle had enough onions, potatoes, turnips, and carrots growing to fill the root cellar come fall. They had twenty calves that fattened up would bring in needed cash. And their meadow had already yielded a good first cutting of hay and might even give a second if the weather held. Putting up enough hay to feed the breeding animals through the winter—that was the key to this country.

Frederik frowned. The few times he'd ridden by the O'Leary place on the creek, he'd seen little evidence of any work being done there. Probably, he thought, that was because Naill O'Leary and Augie were putting all their efforts into sinking a mine deeper and deeper into a mountainside. To Frederik, it seemed a fool thing to do, to chase after gold and let their homestead go uncared for.

But at least the mining kept Augie and Naill away a lot, and they didn't always take Maureen. That left her time for Frederik.

*Maybe I could see her today.* He and Uncle Joe were going to blow some stumps in the afternoon, but after that he might be free to walk down to the creek, and maybe she'd be waiting there. . . .

She would laugh when he told her about the evening before, how he'd tried to play his father's violin.

He was ashamed at how little he remembered. The names of the strings—G, D, A, E—yes, he had those, but he'd had a struggle trying to tune them.

"Perhaps," his uncle had said, listening to Frederik try to pluck them into some kind of harmony, "it would be better with the bow."

But a few moments later, Uncle Joe had to say, "No, I guess not."

*Yes, it would be a funny story to tell Maureen.*

But it was a story that made Frederik regretful, too. There was something about this place and about her that called for music, and he didn't know how to make it.

"NEPHEW, ANOTHER hour of solid work," Uncle Joe said in midafternoon, "and then you go see if there are any fish in the creek." The skin around his eyes wrinkled as he teased, "That *is* why you go down to the creek every chance you get? To look for fish?"

"Absolutely," Frederik answered.

"But meanwhile, will you keep your mind on what you're doing, so that dynamite we're using doesn't blow *us* up!"

They had finished ditch digging for the day and were now clearing some of the upper field that ran along the edge of Joe's property. It would make a good hay field once it was open enough to work with a team, and they already had the irrigation ditch far enough along to get water to it.

Most of the big timber had been taken out of the field long ago, and this past winter they'd cut down what was left, hauling the tree trunks to a sawmill and burning the slash. Now there were just these stumps to be yanked out or blasted with dynamite, and, of course, countless rocks to be loaded onto a rock sled and dragged to the edge.

*Tree stumps and rocks. Those are two things I'm fast becoming an expert on,* Frederik thought. "Ready for me to set the next charge?" he asked.

"Better hold off," his uncle answered. He gestured toward a couple of men down on the road. "It looks like we've got visitors. Want to take a break and say hello?"

THE MEN, a pair of surveyors, were positioning a tripod when Frederik and his uncle got down to them, and one of them explained that they were working on a federal project. "The government wants good surveys of all this land that's not been properly mapped before."

"About time," Uncle Joe said. "We've got one neighbor we'll be glad to show some official survey markers to."

The men laughed, and the one who was doing the speaking said, "We never know when we come onto a place if we're going to be welcomed or shot at, and to tell the truth, your dynamite didn't seem all that friendly until we saw what it was."

"Don't know how we'd settle this country without the stuff," Uncle Joe said. "It's handy."

"Handy and dangerous," the man said. "But I guess about everything you do out here is risky one way or another."

"That it is," Joe agreed. "That it is."

# TESSIE

Things changed after the recital. At school that Monday, I found kids huddled around our teacher, who was showing them the newspaper with my picture in it. "Our celebrity," she said when I entered the room. "I think we should proclaim this Tessie Thaler Day."

Suddenly everybody liked me. A girl named Anne said I was going to be the first person she invited to her birthday party, and another girl, Sandra, asked me to be her friend. She said that since she was going to start piano lessons, we ought to be *best* friends.

At lunch all the kids wanted to sit by me, and a cafeteria aide picked two and told the rest they'd have to wait for another day.

"Who will you pick tomorrow?" someone asked, and I wondered myself.

Except the next day there wasn't quite so much a push to be next to me, and the day after that, everybody wanted to sit next to Brandon Graham, who came to school on crutches from riding his mountain bike no hands, standing up.

Anne did ask me to her birthday party, but I didn't get to go. She held it on a Thursday afternoon when I was to have a violin lesson, and Mom said a party wasn't a good enough reason to change it.

Sandra's birthday wasn't long after that. Her party was on a Saturday, so I could have gone, only she didn't invite me.

I tried not to care, but Dad knew I was disappointed. All that day he did special things with me. We went to a craft store and bought plaster of paris, and then we hiked along a muddy creek bank until we found animal tracks that didn't belong to somebody's dog or cat. "Muskrat," Dad told me.

He showed me how to stir water into plaster until we had a smooth paste just thin enough to pour into the spraddle-toed tracks, and while we waited for the casts to harden he told me how muskrats build burrows and make underwater entrances.

Afterward we went to a park where we sat side by side on swings. The sun had dipped behind the hills by then, and although my sweater kept my arms warm, the air felt chilly on my face.

Dad asked, "Have you got something you want to talk to your old man about?"

"I guess not."

"I'm pretty good at listening."

"I know." My voice sounded little, even to myself.

We swung back and forth while the night got darker. Then I blurted out, "Why am I different?"

Dad asked, "Do you think you are?"

"Other kids think so." I told him about Shawn Peterson calling me a musical freak, and how Anne and Sandra told him he was just jealous. Only I didn't tell Dad that I heard them whispering afterward. Sandra said, "She is pretty weird. My mother says it's not natural for a kid to spend all her time doing one thing."

Dad said, "You haven't told me what you think. Do you believe your violin playing makes you different?"

"Kind of. I'm glad I'm good at my violin, but I don't understand why I'm especially good. It can't just be because I practice."

I tried to think how to explain.

I said, "There's this boy in my class who wants to be a baseball player, a real one, like in the major leagues. All he does every recess is practice throwing, and every night his father takes him to a pitching place where he can work for hours. Only there's another kid just in second grade who's already better."

Dad shook his head. "I don't think anybody understands why some children get one talent and others another, or why an occasional child receives talent in an extraordinary amount."

"Like me?" I asked.

"Like you. The best I can tell you is to think of your

ability with your violin as an unexplained gift to enjoy and be thankful for."

"Because it just is?" I asked.

"Because it just is," he answered.

I had one more question. "Dad, do you wish I didn't have my gift?"

He didn't answer directly. He said, "I would never change who you are."

I didn't like sixth grade, not as long as I was in it.

That was the year I had a teacher named Ms. Watkins, who all the parents tried to get for their kids because she made students work up to their potential. Ms. Watkins didn't put up with nonsense.

So Mom got Ms. Watkins for me and then got into an argument with her the very first day of school. Mom said she'd be picking me up at lunchtime twice a week for violin lessons but would get me back not more than a half hour late. She'd scheduled things that way because my violin teacher that year was a university professor who couldn't fit me in any other time.

"I can't have Tess being tardy on a regular basis," Ms. Watkins said. "I work my pupils hard, and Tess will need to be present if she's not going to get behind."

"I think I know what Tessie needs," Mom told her.

"And I know what my students need."

They took their argument to the principal, who sided with Mom. He told Ms. Watkins that schools must accommodate the requirements of individuals.

Ms. Watkins didn't say another word about it that I knew of. Sometimes, though, when I returned from one of my violin lessons, she'd hold up her hand to stop whatever work was going on. "Tess, just take your time," she'd say.

No, I didn't like sixth grade, and I especially didn't like sixth grade reading, which was one hard book after another. I got Cs and Ds on my quizzes, and Ms. Watkins thought I wasn't taking time to read carefully. "If you didn't have the potential, that would be one thing," she told me. "But you're gifted. A brilliant, gifted student unable to answer simple comprehension questions? Don't try to pull that with me."

I wasn't trying to pull anything. I wasn't brilliant. I wasn't even like the smart kids who were smart in everything. Maybe when I played my violin I was special, but in doing schoolwork I was just average and sometimes not even that.

And while I usually got my homework right, that was often because Mom helped me.

Then one evening my parents went out, and I was left on my own to do a whole fill-in-the-blank page about a book I didn't understand. I wrote in answers the best I could, but I knew I was getting it all wrong.

In school the next morning, which was a Friday, we

exchanged papers for grading. When the kid who did mine called out "fifty-five," several kids giggled, and I heard Sandra say, "And she thinks she's so great." Tears welled in my eyes, and I couldn't blink them away fast enough to keep others from seeing.

Ms. Watkins started the class on a new task and then said, "Tess, let's step into the hall a moment."

Once we were alone, she said, "Tess, you can't continue to focus on only one thing. You need to learn to read well, to learn math, and to learn about the world so that you can find your place in it. You need to put as much effort into other areas of your life as you do into your violin."

She waited for me to answer, but I was afraid I would start really crying if I tried to.

"Do you put your schoolwork first?" she asked. "When you go home in the afternoon, you ought to do your assignments before anything else—telephone, television, computer, violin..."

When I still didn't say anything, she made a little tsking sound. "Maybe I'll call your mother."

That Monday morning Dad caught an early plane to Seattle, to take a class that would keep him away for a couple of weeks. Mom drove him to the airport and got back in time to have breakfast with me. Only then, instead of getting her keys again, she told me I was staying home for the day.

"Why?" I asked.

"Because I want you to. You can study on your own this morning, and after lunch you can practice your violin."

"Why?" I asked again.

"Don't ask *why*, Tessie," she told me. "Just do it. I've got to go out for a while."

She kept me home the next day, also, only this time Mom told me what lessons to do. I did math problems that she checked over, and then she told me to show her where my class was in our social studies book.

"What's going on?" I asked. "Is this about Ms. Watkins's phone call?"

"Tessie, I'm not ready for questions," Mom answered. "I'm just going to do your lessons with you until I can get some things worked out."

Then we read aloud a chapter about agriculture and Mom told me about a summer she'd once spent on a cousin's Ohio farm.

By THURSDAY we had a new routine down, schoolwork in the morning and violin practice most of the afternoon, and Mom still hadn't explained what things she was working out.

Friday morning, instead of opening my books I folded my hands on top of them. "When am I going back to school?" I asked.

"Not today. Please open your reading text."

"Mom, when?"

I could see she didn't want to answer, but I just waited, and finally she said, "You're not. I can teach you better than Ms. Watkins seems able to, and in less time. That will open up hours for your violin."

It took me a moment to realize what Mom was telling me. "Do you mean I'm not ever going back? That I'm going to homeschool?"

"That's exactly what I mean."

*But what about my friends?* I thought. I didn't ask, because Mom might have asked back, *What friends?* and I didn't have any particular ones to name for her.

I considered asking, *But what am I going to do all day?* only there wasn't any point. Mom had already told me. I'd study and I'd practice.

Study and practice.

Practice and practice.

"Tessie, where are you going?" Mom asked.

"To the bathroom," I said, bolting from the table. I had to throw up.

I hung over the toilet bowl gagging while Mom knocked on the locked door. "Tessie, are you all right? Tessie, answer me."

BEGINNING THE DAY I learned I wouldn't be returning to school, I did all my practicing alone in my bedroom. Mom didn't like it, but she let me. Maybe she thought I'd given in all I was going to. Maybe she just figured that even with my bedroom door closed, she'd hear if I stopped working.

I hated Mom for a while, and I wanted to hate my violin. Resenting it was as close as I could get, though, and even that didn't last.

Things were different with my violin now that I was working with it alone. I started thinking of it as a friend, and when I'd go to my room each day after lunch, I'd find it waiting for me.

I didn't hear what Mom said to Dad when he came home from his conferences and learned she'd withdrawn me from school. They took that discussion out of the house. I watched television while they stayed gone for hours and hours. Then late that night, they came into my room and stood at the foot of my bed while I pretended to be asleep.

Dad whispered, "Don't you ever just want to let her be a kid?"

"She's not just a kid," Mom answered.

The next morning Dad asked if the new arrangement was okay with me. "You say the word and we'll get you back in school. And with a different teacher, too."

Mom, scrambling eggs at the stove, said, "We've been over and over this, Stephen."

"Tessie?" Dad asked.

I didn't know what I wanted. I felt odd about not going to school, but I didn't really miss it.

"Tessie?" he repeated. "Don't you want to be with other children? Playing games—soccer or jump rope or whatever kids do now—and having fun?"

"Nobody jumps rope," I said.

"You know, you don't *have* to play your violin just because you can. And you don't have to make it your whole life."

*But it already is,* I thought, and didn't answer him.

Still sounding troubled, Dad said, "Then I guess that's that for now. But remember you can always change your mind."

He told Mom, "And you remember that the violin case stays closed on Saturdays."

A sudden smile replaced some of the concern on his face. "Tessie," he said, "what would you think about going on the Thaler payroll? Saturday mornings at the clinic for five bucks an hour. It would be a regular job, so you'd have to show up."

"I already show up."

"This would make things official. And on Saturday afternoons, maybe once in a while you can treat your old man to ice cream, instead of the other way around. Is it a deal?"

"Deal," I said, relieved to have things settled.

A few weeks later Mr. Capianelli returned to Missoula to give a Christmas concert, and Mom invited him to dinner. I played my violin for him, and he praised how my music had matured. "Although," he said to my parents, "you realize there's a limit to what Tess can do here."

"What do you mean?" Mom asked.

"That Montana, no matter how you look at it, is . . ." He hesitated. "Is a bit provincial. For a serious musician, that is."

"But you said Tessie's music is maturing."

"It is, it is. Just not to the extent that it might if she were in, say, New York. There, her opportunities to hear the best, perhaps to *play* with the best, would be unlimited."

Mom got a faraway look in her eyes. But she laughed. "I'm afraid that's out of the question," she said. "Tessie is very young."

"Out of the question," Dad echoed.

Mr. Capianelli mentioned New York again as he was leaving. Standing in the doorway with his overcoat on, he said, "The time to make things happen for Tess is while she *is* young. Wait too long, and it will be too late."

LATER DAD BUILT a fire in the fireplace. Mom and I poured mugs of hot spiced cider and put on some music.

Instead of taking their usual two chairs, my parents sat close together on the sofa, and Dad put his arm around Mom. Then Mom said, "Mr. Capianelli certainly surprised me with his talk of New York."

I tensed up, sure she was going to ruin the nice mood, but she added, "It's unrealistic, of course."

"It is," Dad said. "And as for hearing good music— how about I stop the CD and you give us some live piano music."

Mom, who rarely touched the piano anymore, took some coaxing, but then she played well, and Dad and I clapped enthusiastically. "You could go onstage, Mom," I said, teasing, wanting to make her happy.

Mom returned to the sofa, snuggling back into Dad's arm. "Not at my age," she said. "Talk about too late."

Her voice took on a musing tone. "Maybe if I'd begun the way you did, but I was in high school before my family even got a piano. Or maybe if I'd had a bit more courage in college...had at least walked into the music building to find out if I belonged there..."

She broke off. "Who am I kidding? I could have started learning piano when I was a toddler and I still wouldn't play the way you play your violin, Tessie."

"Don't sell yourself short," Dad told her. "You're a fine pianist."

"I'm an *amateur* pianist," Mom answered. "I doubt if I'd ever have been more than that no matter what opportunities I was given."

She looked down at her hands, so long boned and slim. "It's different with Tessie," she said. "Sometimes I suspect we still don't grasp how much talent she's got. That's why I'm so afraid we'll do something wrong with it."

"I'm more scared we'll do something wrong with *her*," Dad answered.

"Hey!" I interrupted. "Did you two forget I'm here? I've got some ideas."

Dad and Mom looked startled, but then they laughed. "And what are they?" Dad asked.

"The first is that we go outside and build a snowman."

"It's dark out," Dad protested.

"There's a moon."

"And it's past your bedtime," he said.

"My second idea is that I get to stay up an extra hour."

"I vote with Tessie," Mom said.

We didn't build a snow*man*. We built a snow family that we gave pinecone eyes and our hats. They looked happy. Cold but happy, with their stick arms all interlocked.

January began the arguing months.

Mom spent her afternoons at the library and on the computer and telephone. At dinner she'd tell us what she'd learned. "The schools in New York . . . ," she'd say, or "As to teachers . . . Tessie would have to audition, of course, but . . ."

One night she said, "I got in touch with Mr. Capianelli, and he said he'd be delighted to write recommendation letters for Tessie."

Another night she said, "I know New York is more expensive than Montana, but I could work part-time."

As Dad was doing more and more often, he looked at Mom as though she'd lost her mind. "Do you know how much our lives would change? Don't you understand that my clinic—our livelihood—is here? And even if I could start up in New York, what about Tess? Do you want her growing up in a place without open spaces? Without trees that don't have 'Keep Off' signs on them?"

"A place with art museums and concert halls," Mom said.

"We have those things. And there were reasons we chose to live in Montana and raise Tess here."

"You chose."

Then Mom dropped her voice back, like she really wanted to come to an agreement. "Tessie and I could try it out for a few months. And if we ended up staying, we'd still come home summers and Christmases, and you could do your vacations in New York."

Dad and I stared at her. "You can't be serious," he said.

"Mom, no," I told her.

JANUARY SLIPPED into February which became March while Mom intensified her arguments and Dad dug in his heels.

Mostly I stayed out of it, practicing my violin so loudly that I couldn't hear either of them. Also, I practiced because it was one thing I loved to do.

That and my job at Dad's clinic on Saturdays. I loved doing that, too, and I had a lot of fun deciding how to use the money I earned. I bought CDs and saved toward new hiking boots. A few times I rented ice skates and tried to blend in with the crowd of kids darting about the town rink.

Then April came, and the arguments ranged further. Dad seemed to be struggling to hang on to ground that he was becoming less and less sure of. Mom's California upbringing came into the arguments, and I heard her tell Dad, "Stephen, I've given your precious Montana a try. There's not enough for me here, any more than there is for Tessie."

I wanted to curl up in my closet, but I didn't. I settled near a door from where I wouldn't miss hearing anything, because I knew more was being discussed than just Montana.

"Any child belongs with her family," Dad said.

"I've told you and told you Tessie isn't just any child," Mom said. "Don't you want what's best for her?"

Later that evening, when Mom and I were alone, she said to me, "Tessie, I just want you to try New York. If you're unhappy, we won't stay. But if you don't give it a try, you'll never know what you could have done there."

As May went by and then June, it seemed as if every part of my life was being weighed; as if each piece was being put on one side or the other of an old-time balance scale. Dad and the clinic and my home went on one side, along with exploring in the woods and living in the only town I'd ever known.

On the other side of the scale there was just Mom and my violin and a chance to learn music the way people like Mr. Capianelli said I ought to. Just those three, but in the end they seemed to weigh more than everything else.

Mom called a travel agent and booked one-way tickets to New York.

# TESS

By late afternoon we've gained enough altitude that we're hiking through a rocky, subalpine terrain of low grasses. There are still trees, but they're not as big as the ones lower down. Amy starts asking, "How much farther?" and Dad answers, "We're almost there."

Then we reach a place where the trail runs directly below the mountain's highest point, and another twenty minutes of climbing up a narrow, branching path takes us to the rock-strewn top of Stuart Peak. A chain of blue-green lakes stretches off in one direction, and the Missoula valley lies in the other. And on all sides, mountains, layers on layers of them, stretch into the distance.

"Wow!" Amy exclaims, and Meg murmurs, "Oh, my."

It's so lovely it brings tears to my eyes, the way unexpected music sometimes does. In fact, it doesn't take much effort to imagine music in the wind's sound as it blows across the exposed peak. We pass around binoculars and take pictures until the wind picks up strong enough to make us want our sweatshirts, which we've left with our gear down on the trail.

"It's time we were making camp, anyway," Dad says without lowering his binoculars. He's looking in the direction where we'll be hiking tomorrow. "Jake Randall and his wife are coming this way. I'd know his neon yellow backpack anywhere."

"Who's Jake Randall?" I ask.

"A bird guy—ornithologist—from the university. They left a few days ago to hike the loop we're doing but in the opposite direction." Dad turns to Meg. "I told Jake about the gulch where you hope to locate that old homestead. His wife's a history buff."

Amy, tagging on my heels as we head down off the peak, says, "I hope those people go someplace else. It's supposed to be just *us* camping."

Surprised, I realize I was thinking the same thing.

WE SET UP on a gentle slope below the ridgeline. Dad takes our water filter and empty water bottles down to the nearest lake, Meg starts dinner, and Amy and I haul out the tents.

The ground is lumpy with stones and clump grass, but we eventually find two fairly flat spots. And aside from Amy almost poking my eye out before she gets the hang of snapping poles together, the tent setup goes pretty smoothly.

"Done!" I say, admiring Dad and Meg's blue tunnel tent and Amy's and my new green dome.

Amy, though, gets paper and a pencil from her mom's pack to make a sign for ours: TESS AND AMY'S TENT. PRIVATE! STAY OUT!!

Laughing, I tell her, "That's probably not necessary."

"We don't want any boys coming in."

"What boys?"

"In case," she says, placing the page at the tent door like an unwelcome mat and anchoring it with a stone. "Or anybody. Do you have a boyfriend?"

"You're not *too* curious!" I tell her.

"Well, do you?"

"Kind of." *I don't know, not anymore.* "A guy named Ben."

"Ben that's in the magazine picture?"

"That's him, the cello player."

I expect Amy to ask what I meant by "kind of," but instead she says, "I'm glad he's not a total boyfriend, or else you'd miss him."

"I do miss him," I tell her.


WE HAVE SPAGHETTI, all of us eating like we're starved. Then the Randalls walk in and Dad introduces us. When Dad gets to me, Dr. Randall says, "The famous violinist."

After they set up their tents, the Randalls join us

again, bringing along marshmallows for the hot chocolate Meg makes.

We drink it watching the sky change colors where the
sun has set. It's going on ten o'clock. That's something I'd
forgotten, how long daylight lasts in a Montana summer.

When the talk turns to Meg's project, Myrna Randall
says, "We spent some time exploring the gulch you're interested in. We wanted to surprise you with something
helpful, but we didn't see so much as a piece of old
barbed wire."

"I'd be surprised if you had," Meg tells her. "The forest covers things up pretty well."

"I know, but we had hopes. We even climbed up to a
rock ledge thinking it would give us a vantage point from
where we might spot the outline of something."

"But you didn't?"

"The only straight lines we saw were tree trunks."

Dr. Randall puts his cup down. "I hate to be the one
to break this up, but we need to turn in. Myrna and I
have to hit the trail early." He pauses before adding,
"Stephen, I meant to say that I'm sorry about your owl.
Tough news."

I'm sitting near enough to Dad that I'm aware of him
bracing himself as he asks, "What news was that?"

"Didn't Fish and Wildlife call? Someone found that
great horned owl you took care of—"

"Midnight."

"—by the side of the highway last week. He apparently got into some poison that killed him."

"I don't believe you," Amy cries.

Meg asks, "Are you sure it was Midnight?"

"They'd have known," Dad says, his voice flat. "His leg band would have ID'd him. Poison..." He shakes his head once, quickly.

Amy jumps up. "I hate you," she yells at Dr. Randall. Then she runs to our tent, and after a moment Meg goes after her.

I follow Dad to an overlook above the dark chain of lakes and valley.

"I'm sorry about Midnight," I tell him.

Dad is quiet a long time, but just when I decide he's not going to answer, he says, "I wonder what the point is. Midnight's not the first animal I've patched up only to have it get killed in a world that has less and less space for wild things."

"You're not thinking about stopping rehab work, are you?"

"Sometimes I'm tempted."

"But you've spent all these years learning how to do it," I say. "You can't just *not* use what you know."

Dad shoots me an odd look. "I said *tempted.* No, I won't quit. The successes are too precious."

This time the silence stretches out even longer, until I say, "Amy sounded pretty upset."

"I know." Dad sighs. "It's harder seeing your kids

hurt than it is being hurt yourself. You ache for them, and you wonder what you could have done differently."

A little later, when we see Meg stirring, he asks, "Ready to go down?"

"I'll stay up here a bit," I answer.

I stay a long time, thinking and remembering. Wondering if there was anything Dad would do differently for himself.

I think of the comment his assistant, Janie, made about how Dad's rehab work wasn't what paid the bills. Maybe she was referring to how much it costs to keep me in New York, in my academic school and in music school. Mom's salary doing public relations for a museum doesn't begin to cover it all, but I've never heard Dad complain.

But would he give up some of his pet-care work if we didn't need all the income it brings in?

And what Dad said about parents aching for their kids. Was he talking just about Amy, or about me, too? And if it was me, did he mean me now or when I was her age?

I gaze out over the valley below, wishing I could find answers in its calm. Except of course I know the valley's not really as still as it looks.

Right this minute bears are roaming down there, raccoons and bobcats are starting rounds of nighttime hunting, deer and elk are bedding down, and beavers are gliding along creeks.

I can picture the valley a couple of months from now, on a day bright with the glow of a larch yellow autumn. And I can imagine how, after that, it will become a winter white landscape of snow and ice. And each animal will know what it's supposed to do to get through the cold months.

They won't all make it. Some will freeze or starve, and some will know moments of panic when predators close in. But at least they won't have spent their lives worrying and planning and wondering what they're supposed to do next.

I DON'T COME down from the overlook until several stars appear. Returning to camp, I see Dad and Meg sitting with their arms linked, their heads touching.

"Good night," I call softly.

I try not to listen in on their conversation as I go by, but their voices carry. I hear Meg say, "Surely taking care of Midnight can't have been anything *but* right. All you can do for any creature is give it a chance."

"And your heart breaks for them when they don't make it," Dad answers.

Amy is asleep in our tent, taking her half out of the middle. I tug her, sleeping bag and all, over to one side. I don't think I've woken her, but a few moments after I settle into my own sleeping bag, she says, in a voice so low I can hardly hear her, "I'm never going to help Pop with another animal. It was my fault Midnight died."

"That's not true!"

"Yes, it is. We got him well and put his cage in the pickup and drove into the woods, and then Pop asked me where I thought we should let Midnight go. And I pointed to some trees because I thought Midnight would like being able to see the river from them."

Amy starts crying. "Pop said I'd picked the perfect spot, only I didn't. I picked a spot where there was poison."

I reach over, find her hand in her sleeping bag, and squeeze it. "You had no way of knowing that. Besides, Midnight might have found the poison miles away from where you left him."

"If I'd picked better, he never would have."

"Maybe not," I tell her. "But if you hadn't taken a chance and picked *some* place, he'd still be in a cage. Is that what you'd want for him?"

"No." Amy sniffs, and her sobs lessen.

"You and Dad did your best for Midnight. You patched him up, and you gave him a chance to live his own life again. So you did right. Okay?"

"Okay," Amy answers. She pulls her hand from mine. "But I'm still done taking care of things."

The next thing I know, it's early morning, and sunlight is pricking through the mosquito netting on the tent door. If I half close my eyes, I can see patterns in the sparkles of light: a grid like a ticktacktoe game and a leaf and a spray of flowers. I feel lazy and comfortable enough that I'd like to stay in my sleeping bag, but I can hear the others already getting breakfast.

Amy chatters too brightly as we take down our tent and stuff our sleeping bags into their sacks. She goes on about everything except Midnight.

Today's goal is one of the lakes in the long chain of high mountain lakes that we saw from the top of Stuart Peak.

Amy runs ahead, dashes off the trail, pops up behind us, and, generally, does her best to make a nuisance of herself.

"You're going to wear yourself out," Meg tells her.

Dad, scouting for interesting birds to watch, is hiking up where our talking won't make him miss hearing them. Now, though, he calls to Amy to look through his binoculars at an eagle soaring high overhead.

She ignores him and dashes into the woods again, and the next time she reappears, Meg tells her, "Calm down now, Amy. I do not want you out of sight."

"Okay!" Amy says, "but I don't see why." She hurries to put some distance between her and us, and then she settles into a defiant stride.

"She was pretty upset about Midnight," I say.

"I know," Meg answers. "But I don't know what to do except let her be for now. Sometimes people need time to lick their wounds the way animals do."

THE TRAIL ENTERS a sloping mountain meadow dotted with red paintbrush and small yellow flowers like daisies. The morning sun gives the hillsides a golden hue, and above them the sky is deep blue and cloudless.

"Did you ever see a prettier day?" Meg asks. "I hope this weather holds. It's perfect for hiking, and it will make the working part of our trip easier."

"It would have been nice if the Randalls had spotted something helpful," I say.

"I'm just as glad they didn't," Meg replies. "They might not have known not to disturb things. It's a perennial problem—someone finds an object of historic interest and carts it away to display on a coffee table. Or maybe even brings it to my office thinking they're doing a good deed."

"Like the guy with the kettle."

"Yep. What people don't realize is that when you remove an object from its context, you destroy much of its value as an artifact that can help explain the site."

Meg gives me a wry smile. "What they also don't realize is that removing artifacts like old tools and cabin hardware can be a violation of both the Antiquities Act and the laws against taking things from federal land."

I say, "What I don't get is why you're setting out on foot, without equipment, to find this place. Isn't there technology to help? I read about how people used aerial photography and infrared film to find fire rings along Lewis and Clark's route."

"That kind of archaeology takes money, so you have to set priorities," Meg says. "The journey made by Lewis and Clark was unique in our country's history, while there were probably hundreds of homesteads like the Bottners'. Thousands, maybe."

"Then why do you want to find it?"

"Because it might fill in a little of the story of what happened here in western Montana. In the 'Snake, especially."

"So what do you do? Just walk around and hope to come across something?"

Meg laughs. "With any archaeological project, the work starts with learning all you can of an area's history. Then once you're in the field, you still have to work from a grasp of what time does to artifacts and structures—how it deteriorates some things faster than others, and how it lays down soil until the past is compressed in the layers beneath your feet."

"That you work through backward?"

"That you work through backward," Meg agrees. "And then whatever you find has to be interpreted. That's where the real skill comes in, and where one historian's work gets separated from another's."

"Music's that way," I say. "The actual music that a composer writes doesn't change, but every musician interprets it a little differently."

"I wouldn't have thought of that analogy, but it's a good one." Meg gives me a grin. "I've talked your ear off, haven't I?"

"No," I tell her. "I was interested. You really love it, don't you? Your work, I mean."

"I do," she says. "I surely do."

We're slow to put our packs on after a midmorning break, and I'm not the only one who groans a little.

"The second day out is always the hardest," Dad says. And truly, I'm pretty uncomfortable, with leg muscles that remember yesterday's climb, and half the bugs in Montana taking turns sliding down my sweaty neck.

Amy's still acting silly, only she's walking with me now instead of keeping to herself. In fact, she's walking almost on my heels, and when I ask her to drop back she moves closer and tries to bring her toe down on the back of my boot.

"Amy, quit it," I tell her.

"Bet you can't make me," she says, darting around me.

"I said—" I break off, puzzled by a strange sound. "Hush," I say, grabbing her arm. "Did you hear that?"

"What?" she asks, pulling free.

Then I hear it again, a breathy cough.

"Dad!" I say, glad he and Meg are only a few feet in front. "I think I hear an animal. Something big."

Dad's hand goes to the canister of hot-pepper spray that hangs from his pack belt. "Where?"

"Up ahead, just past where the trail bends."

An instant later Meg says, "Look in that tree." She points to a ball of black fur—a bear cub—clinging to a high limb. "We sure don't want to get between it and its mama!"

We go back the way we came, and once we're a safe distance away, Dad says, "It's a good thing you heard that mother bear's warning, Tess. That could have been nasty."

Meg nods, her hand firmly clamped on Amy's shoulder.

"I KNEW IT was a bear," Amy says. She's walking with me again as Dad and Meg lead us on a wide detour around the cub and its mom. "Or I would have, if I'd heard it cough."

"How?" I ask.

"Because I know a cough is a bear sound. They've got a lot of different ones, but a cough—it's called a huff—that's one of their warnings that they don't like what's going on. Like standing on their hind legs is another." Amy becomes animated as she tells me what she knows. "A huff's different from a growl, which bears do when they're fighting. And when they just whimper—that's a mother bear calling her cubs."

"Where'd you learn all that?" I ask. "Did Dad teach you?"

"I guess."

"Do you know as much about the animals he has at the clinic?"

Amy's face turns expressionless. "I told you, I'm not doing the clinic anymore. I don't care about any old animals."

Then she rushes ahead to a fallen tree that lies at an angle, its roots still partly in the ground and its needled top several feet up in the air. She jumps onto the low end and begins walking up its trunk, arms out to steady herself. "Look at me," she calls. "I'm on a balance beam."

"Amy!" Meg exclaims as she and Dad and I hurry to get under her. "Come down now, before you fall and break a leg!"

"Why?" Amy asks. "I can do this. I'm surefooted." The edge of her backpack snags a branch, and she bobbles but catches herself. She says, "See!"

"Now!" Dad says, reaching an arm up to her. Amy hesitates, and then, making a face, jumps down on the other side. The weight of her backpack sends her sprawling, and she scrambles up red-faced but unhurt except for some scratches.

"Amy," Meg tells her, "you will either behave or walk with me until you're ready to."

I hear Amy mutter, "You're not the boss of me."

"What did you say?" Meg asks.

"Nothing."

"Yes, she is," I whisper.

AMY STOMPS along in injured silence for a good five minutes before blurting out, "They think I'm a baby!" She pushes through some brush and lets the branches snap back. One just misses my face.

"Hey!" I protest. "Watch it."

"It's true. Everything fun, Mom says I'm too little for. She's always *deciding* things for me!"

"She's your mom. What do you expect?"

Amy kicks a pinecone so hard it bounces off the rock that it hits. "Do people decide stuff for you?"

"Yeah."

"Did somebody decide for you to come to Montana?"

"No. My mother didn't want me to do that."

"Then what?"

I think a moment, trying to pick one example from dozens I could give her. "Well, it was other people's decision when I moved to New York with Mom."

"Moving doesn't count. Kids never get a say in that," Amy says. Then she asks, "Didn't you want to go?"

"Not really. I was pretty scared."

"You're not supposed to let people make you do things you're scared of. Mom says when you're scared there's usually a good reason, and you'd better figure out what it is before you get talked into doing something stupid."

I hold back a smile. "It was mainly my mom saying we should go."

"Moms aren't always right," she says, totally ignoring the fact she's just been quoting her own. She picks up another pinecone, which she tries to kick like a Hacky Sack. "And you shouldn't have to mind moms when they're not."

"Oh?" I say, feeling a twinge of sympathy for Meg. For Dad, too, since Amy is half his responsibility now.

Amy's face puckers with earnestness. "Like you. You went to New York 'cause your mom said to, and that's how you ended up at that concert, right? The one where you played so bad? But then she said not to come out here and you did anyway, and it's perfect."

I feel my face grow hot. It hadn't occurred to me that Amy knew about the concert. I suppose Dad or Meg told her hoping she wouldn't ask embarrassing questions.

"I'm glad you're here," Amy says. "I don't want you to ever go back."

"Are you sure? You hardly know me."

She retrieves the pinecone, tosses it up, and manages to boot it three times before it drops. "Yes, I do. So will you? Promise to stay forever and ever?"

"I can't promise that."

"At least for the rest of high school?"

"Maybe. I can't promise."

"You better!" Amy scoops up a green caterpillar.

"Because if you don't, I'll put this down your neck!" She snatches at my shirt collar.

"Okay, I give you my word," I say, scrambling out of reach. "But my fingers are crossed."

"I don't believe in crossed fingers. So now you've promised!"

"No, I didn't."

Amy puts down the caterpillar and then pauses to examine a millipede. "I don't think these things actually have a whole thousand legs," she says. "Fifty, maybe. So, was New York really bad?"

"No. I didn't like it at first—Manhattan is about as different from Missoula, Montana, as you can imagine—but once I got over feeling lost, it was okay."

"Because you got a boyfriend, right?" Amy asks. "Ben?"

"No. Before that," I tell her.

"Then what made you like it?" she asks.

I think back. "Lots of things. But the first... There was a cello player."

"That's what I *said*. Ben, right?"

"No, no. This was a different person altogether. Just someone I heard play once."

"Was he good?"

"Very."

# TESSIE

New York. I'd known it was big, but I still didn't expect the jumbling, towering, rushing, squishing-in size of it. Nor the noise—the sirens and horns, the belch of bus exhausts and the rumbling roar of subways beneath my feet. Sound after sound startled me my first days there, and I wanted to cling to Mom's hand like I was a little kid instead of a twelve-year-old girl.

"You'll get used to it," Mom told me. "In no time you'll feel at home."

I figured I'd get over being frightened, but I doubted I'd ever be at home in a place so different from what I was used to. Even the air felt different, hot and sticky right through the night. Where I was from, no matter how hot August got, things cooled down at night.

And I didn't like looking up at buildings instead of sky. I missed mountains. I missed Dad. I missed living in a house big enough that I could go off by myself when I wanted to.

The apartment Mom and I moved into just had a bathroom and two rooms: a tiny one that Mom took for hers and a midsize one that served for everything else. One end was the kitchen; one end had windows that looked out on a street always jammed with traffic; and the space in between was both our living room and, with the sofa folded out, my bedroom.

Mom stayed away for hours every day arranging things like telephone service and finding out where to buy groceries and how to cope with getting them home without a car. I'd have gone with her if she'd let me, but she said I needed to prepare for meeting my new violin teacher.

I tried, but for the first time in years I practiced with an eye on the clock, wishing for a morning or afternoon to end. I felt disconnected from my violin, and I felt shut in by the little apartment with its windows closed against street noises. More and more I wished we hadn't left Montana.

Finally I got up my nerve to say, "I don't like it here. I want to go home."

"Please trust me, Tessie," Mom said. "You'll feel different after your lessons start. And you're going to love Manhattan. There's so much here."

"I haven't seen anything," I told her. "You don't even let me leave the apartment."

"That's just for now, until I can teach you how to get around." Mom squeezed my shoulders. "What would you think about taking the day off? I saw an ad for tours of Lincoln Center. We could see where some of the best music in the world gets played."

"Will there be a concert?" I asked.

"Not on a Saturday morning, but we can get a sense of the center. After all, maybe one day you'll play there."

"Mom..."

"I said *maybe*. Right now we'll just go enjoy ourselves, like any other tourists."

I WAS SURPRISED to find that Lincoln Center wasn't one huge auditorium, the way I'd pictured, but several buildings. The three biggest were huge, glass-fronted halls that each faced one side of a great plaza with a fountain in its middle. Banners proclaimed the hall on the left to be home of the New York City Ballet and the New York City Opera. The building at the back of the U was the Metropolitan Opera House, and our guide said the American Ballet Theatre also performed there.

"The largest venue in Lincoln Center, it seats four thousand nineteen," our guide told us in the droning tones of memorized spiel. "Performers sing without the aid of microphones."

I asked, "Is that where the New York Philharmonic Orchestra plays?"

The guide frowned at being interrupted. "Of course not. The symphony plays in the symphony hall. Avery Fisher Hall. That's next."

I didn't know exactly what I hoped to find in the symphony hall, but its vast space was disappointingly empty except for a woman distributing papers among music stands.

And then a man carrying a cello walked out. He sat down before one of the stands and began playing all by himself, drawing out notes so clear and pure it didn't seem possible that a person was playing them.

Nothing on any CD I'd ever heard and nothing anyone had ever told me had prepared me for the sound of a master musician playing live in a hall built for a symphony.

And Mom...Mom reached over and took my hand.

The first week in September, Mom and I took a bus up Broadway and then walked a couple of blocks over to meet Mr. Geisler in his studio on the upper West Side. Since he'd agreed to take me as a pupil on Mr. Capianelli's recommendation, I guess I expected him to be like Mr. Capianelli. Not in appearance, of course, but in directing most of his talk to Mom, as though they were conspirators who between them would see I benefited from my lessons.

The man who greeted us, violin in hand, was seventy or maybe even eighty. White haired and welcoming, he made it seem like meeting me was the best thing he had going all day. He was nice to Mom, too, but he made it clear that I was the one he'd been waiting for.

"So," he said, "so, my old pupil has sent me his best pupil. Come, let's make some music."

During that first lesson, that's all we did. Mr. Geisler and I played together, moving from one piece to another as I tried to match my playing to his. Somehow he knew what music would be in my repertoire, so I never had to say stop, I don't know that.

I played while listening to our paired violins and watching his face. Occasionally I'd see his eyebrows twitch, and then I'd hear why and make an adjustment. And then the twitching would stop and his eyes would twinkle. Once the twitching got so furious before I could figure out the reason for it that I burst out laughing and lost my place altogether.

When the doorbell announced his next student, I think Mr. Geisler hated ending my lesson as much as I did.

"Thank you," I told him. "Thank you very much."

Mom, whom I'd pretty much forgotten, asked somewhat stiffly, "Have you an assignment for Tessie?"

"I suppose I should," Mr. Geisler said, and I really do think his eyes twinkled at Mom. "Maybe...Here."

He took my right hand, which still held my violin bow, and nudged my fingers into a different position. Gently molding the way my hand was arched, he said, "Now that you're playing a full-size instrument, you might give this grip a try. Work on it, and then next time we can decide if it's an improvement."

The new bow grip led to days of bad playing. It felt awkward to me, and the sounds that came from my violin were so disappointing that I was sure I was doing something wrong. Mom could hear I'd regressed, too, and she moved about our apartment with her lips pressed together.

And then, at the end of a morning I'd spent frustrated and half-panicked at hearing myself play worse and worse, the mail brought a card from Mr. Geisler. It showed a cartoonish robin fighting to pull an impossibly long worm from the ground. The caption underneath said, "Sometimes the hardest struggle comes just before success."

I couldn't believe it. Mr. Geisler knew what a hard time I was having? He knew how I *felt*?

I went back to my practicing determined to keep trying, and, sure enough, late that afternoon I was rewarded with a tone so light and sweet, so crystal-edged, that I knew I was doing what Mr. Geisler wanted me to. And I knew why.

My lessons with Mr. Geisler that winter sparkled like bright patches amid days that otherwise felt as drab as New York clothes.

Mr. Geisler taught me the way my very first teacher, Mr. Dreyden, had, insisting that I understand that *to play* meant I should have fun as well as make music. "Don't take yourself so seriously," he told me. "Music's to be enjoyed!"

He made me laugh at myself. "What?!" he'd demand, when I'd lose control of a rapid piece. "Have you a bow arm or a flapping turkey wing?!"

But we worked hard, too, and we had a goal in sight: my audition for acceptance into one of the world's most renowned music schools. Kids came from all over to study there, and many famous musicians traced their training to it.

Just getting accepted for an audition was a job in itself, but Mom took care of that, filling out forms, gathering recommendations, and recording the required tape of me playing. Mr. Geisler and I concentrated on making sure that when I did get an audition date—he wouldn't let me doubt that I'd be given one—I'd be ready.

I wouldn't only have to show that I played well. I'd also have to demonstrate that I already had command of a basic repertoire of classical pieces. And I'd have to be able to play them completely from memory, too. It was a huge amount to learn, and once I started attending a public junior high, I had fewer hours to practice.

The junior high was more of Mr. Geisler's doing.

When I mentioned I wasn't in school, he questioned Mom about it. She gave him a vague explanation without mentioning the limbo of my school status. As far as the state of Montana knew, I was still living in Missoula and being homeschooled. And as for New York—nobody in that system even knew I was there.

"But what about her meeting other young people?" Mr. Geisler asked. "Tess needs more than music."

"I just don't think this is the time," Mom countered.

At my next lesson, Mr. Geisler brought it up again. This time he said, "You realize that if Tess isn't comfortable playing in a group, it will hurt her chances of being admitted to music school. She needs some orchestral experience."

I didn't know whether that was what convinced Mom or if she gave in because it was the only thing that made sense once she found a job. Anyway, in late February, the same week that Mom mailed my completed music school application, she enrolled me in a junior high that had a small school orchestra.

It was a pretty pathetic ensemble, made up mainly of bored students who didn't particularly want to be in it. The weary teacher, tuning stringed instruments for a line of kids who couldn't tell an A from an A-flat, looked as if he didn't much like conducting it, either.

I concentrated on following his baton and tried not to let my playing stand out, but it did, anyway. After my first orchestra practice, some kids came up to ask how I'd gotten so good.

"It's just that I've been playing since I was three," I said, embarrassed. "Almost three and a half."

"Three?" one of the girls exclaimed. "Did someone make you? Because that would be child abuse or something." Then she and the others moved off, giggling.

I told myself it didn't matter; that I didn't need friends, anyway. That hadn't changed just because I was in New York instead of Montana.

Besides, when I answered Mom's questions about how the junior high was, she said she'd start looking for a place where music was appreciated.

Then one April day a letter arrived from the music school inviting me to an audition the following month. After that, there wasn't time for thinking about anything except getting ready.

Mom went with me, and she seemed as tightly wound as I felt. All the way on the bus, I gripped the handle of my violin case with a hand clammy with sweat.

A woman just inside the school's main door took my name and consulted a clipboard. "The violin faculty is expecting you, Tess." She gave us a room number and directions for getting to it. "You'll find chairs set up in the hall where you can wait until you're called. Good luck!"

As Mom and I made our way down the corridor, I tried not to stare at the scattered parent-kid pairs huddled outside closed doors. Some of the kids looked older than me; some younger. One boy who nervously tapped a flute inside an open case couldn't have been more than seven or eight.

After Mom and I made a wrong turn, a really nice guy about my age, wearing jeans and a T-shirt and carrying a cello, walked us to the right place. "It won't be bad," he told me. "Just play the way you practice."

"Have you already had your audition?" I asked.

"I'm already a student here," he answered. "Just in to do some make-up work." And he wished me good luck.

THE NEXT HOUR went by in a confusion of impressions:

Mom and me sitting on folding metal chairs.

A door down the corridor opening and a girl coming out with tears running down her face.

Other kids and parents searching for audition rooms, the parents' assessing eyes sweeping across my instrument case. The kids' more furtive glances.

Faint sounds of solo music wafting from almost soundproof rooms.

How my hands wouldn't stay still, and how Mom told me to stop shredding a tissue; I was making a mess.

Then the door where we waited opened. A boy exited and a man told me to come in. Mom stood up with me, but he said, "Mrs. Thaler? Please wait here."

Inside the audition room, my accompanist—a woman I'd had just one session with—was seated at a piano. Another woman welcomed me and said not to be nervous. "Take your time tuning and warming up," she told me.

How many teachers were there? Did they all introduce themselves? When Mom asked me later, I couldn't tell her because I didn't remember.

I didn't remember any of the rest of my audition except that I closed my eyes and played straight through everything I'd prepared.

Oh, and I remember that when I was done, the woman who'd welcomed me asked to hear a Pierre Rode étude.

I looked at her blankly.

"You don't know Rode?" she said.

Someone said something in a low tone. And then the same man who'd ushered me into the room saw me out. "Thank you for giving us a chance to hear you," he said.

He told Mom, "You'll receive notice of our decision within three or four weeks."

EXACTLY THREE weeks later, I got the music school's letter. I didn't want to open it, I was so afraid it would be bad news. But I did and saw a sentence that began, "It is with pleasure..."

"Mom!" I said. "Mom. I'm in! I'm *in*. I start in September."

I took the letter to my next lesson, and Mr. Geisler was so happy for me. "Congratulations! I wouldn't have expected any other outcome from your audition, but still it's an accomplishment to be very proud of."

"Now that I've been admitted, I'm a little scared about whether I'll be good enough," I told him.

"You'll do fine."

I thought of the Rode études. "But if the school expects me to know stuff I haven't had yet, you'll help me learn it?"

"Your new teacher will."

"My new teacher? What do you mean?"

Mr. Geisler shot Mom a questioning glance. Then he told me, "When you start music school, a member of the violin faculty will take you on as a student."

"But won't you still be my teacher, also?"

"That's not the way it works," he said. "I thought you understood that. Didn't you read the music school's literature?"

*No!* I thought. *Mom told me what was in it. She must have "forgotten" what I wouldn't want to hear.*

Feeling betrayed and furious, I told her, "I can't believe you kept that from me. I don't want to go to music school if it means giving up Mr. Geisler."

"Don't be ridiculous," Mom said. "Of course you do."

I swung around to face Mr. Geisler. "You should have told me."

"Tess, I'd have to send you to another teacher before long, anyway. You've already learned most of what I can teach you."

"That's not right," I argued. "I'm learning a lot from you."

Smiling slightly, he said, "I hope so. But you need more. Including perhaps a more disciplined approach to your training than mine."

"I like how you do things."

"Come, Tess," he said. "Let's just play for fun today. Then next week we'll buckle down to see how much we can get done in the time we still have together."

MR. GEISLER remained my teacher through the end of June, when I left to spend two months in Montana. The lessons became intense as he readied me for a summer of working on my own. We both knew I'd have to keep up my skills if I wanted to be at my best come fall.

But the lessons were bittersweet, too, because of our awareness that he was preparing me to leave him. One day I tried to say how sad I felt about that, but he wouldn't let me.

"Learning to say good-bye is part of growing up, Tess," he told me. "That's true whatever you do with your life, although maybe it's especially true for some people in some walks of life." He briefly rested his hand on my shoulder. "I'm afraid it's a lesson you have to relearn occasionally, no matter how old you get."

# FREDERIK
## 1907–1908

After being left unplayed for so long—the better part of a year had gone by since Frederik's one attempt—the violin's strings lay dully out of tune. Gingerly, afraid he'd break something, Frederik tightened them to match the tones of his new pitch pipe.

"A birthday present for you, nephew," Uncle Joe had said, tossing it to him on his return from town the evening before.

"But my birthday was in early February."

"Two months ago, I remember, and it was the second time you marked it alone. It'll be the last, though, if the new pasture makes this place finally pay for itself. Then I can give up trapping, except maybe to run a short line to teach you a few more tricks."

Uncle Joe had shaken out his oiled slicker, making water fly across the room. "Anyway, I hope you're still wanting to play that fiddle."

Frederik did. Alone now, though, even with the violin tuned, he wasn't sure how to begin.

He tried the bow on the D string and made a noise that caused the cat, Red, to lay back its ears. He'd forgotten how hard it was to pull the bow smoothly and not let it skitter toward the fingerboard. Finally, though, after loosening his grip and changing the angle, he produced a reasonably even tone.

Over and over he played it, wanting his hand and arm to memorize the feel.

*All right,* he thought. *Now for the next note.*

By pressing the first finger of his left hand tightly against the violin's fingerboard, he shortened the part of the string that the bow could set vibrating. It gave him a note that was higher—not exactly an E, but very close, and with some experimenting he got it sounding right.

The next note he tried, played by pressing his second finger down, was less successful, but he could almost hear his father saying, "Frederik, give attention. The D scale has two sharps: F-sharp and C-sharp." He slid his finger higher to find the first sharp.

His third finger produced a G.

*Come on,* he thought. *I can't play Maureen a song with just those notes.*

He moved his bow across the open A string and played it and then repeated the fingering pattern to get B, C-sharp, and then another, higher, D. An octave! Low D to high D.

"Hey!" he exclaimed so loudly that the cat sprang to its feet. "Sorry, Red."

Within a couple of hours, Frederik was working the notes into simple melodies. Then his uncle came in with mail he'd fetched from town.

"Listen," Joe said, and he read aloud a typed letter filled with phrases like "unauthorized usage." He said, "Of course there's a mistake in the railroad's records. I've told them that. But I'd better write again with the particulars of my deed of sale."

"Do you think the railroad people will believe you?" Frederik asked.

"They'd better. Meanwhile, the first chance I get I'll ride to town to see the land locator who handled this place when the Middlers sold it to me. He knows whose land this is."

"I could go with you," Frederik offered.

Joe laughed. "And, I suppose, take Maureen along, so you can treat her to a soda and a ride in one of those horse-pulled streetcars?" His voice turned serious again. "Nephew, sixteen is still too young to be in love, and Naill O'Leary might not like you courting his daughter. Especially not behind his back."

"I'm not *courting* her," Frederik protested. "There's nothing for him to mind."

"How about when he finds out how much time you're together, not courting?"

Frederik spread out a blanket while Maureen unpacked a picnic lunch of elk sausage, biscuits, and huckleberry pie. The day was a double celebration— Maureen's sixteenth birthday and two years exactly since the September day they'd first met.

They'd walked a long time to get to this spot by a huge old ponderosa, but it commanded a view into the autumn valley that was better for the effort of reaching it.

Taking a bite of sausage, Frederik said, "This is good. Did you make it?"

Maureen nodded. "And I put up the huckleberries, too. I've done all the cooking since…for a long time."

A distance *karoom* rocked the air, followed by a pair of smaller shocks. "That must be Pa and Augie working at the mine," Maureen said. "It's all Pa can think about these days, especially now the government's saying we don't even own our place on the creek."

Frederik turned to look at her. "It's not right that you have to do all the work that gets done there."

"I don't mind," Maureen answered, and then rushed her next words. "I know what people in town say about us. About my mother because she ran off the way she did, and about my father because they think his bad temper was what made her leave. But he didn't used to be angry all the time, and I remember her teaching me nice things."

"Like what?" Frederik asked. "Besides how to cook?"

"Oh ... like how to make things pretty. I just finished making a candleholder—just a tin can, but I punched a pattern of holes in it the way my mother showed me. It shines so nice when a candle's lit inside!"

She bit her lip and then seemed to come to a decision. "Pa and Augie are staying at the mine tonight, so if you'd like to go back with me to our place later on, I can show you."

THE CANDLE FLICKERING in the punched can did make a pretty picture for Frederik and Maureen to look at while they ate. They finished supper—more elk sausage and the end of the pie—and then a quiet fell between them as they faced each other across the table.

It seemed strange to Frederik to be here with Maureen—this was the first time that he'd actually been inside her house. The fact of being here, though, wasn't enough to account for the hot and cold feelings running through him.

"Maureen," he began, hardly knowing how he intended to continue. The door being thrown open interrupted him.

Frederik recognized Maureen's brother against the backlight in the instant before Augie lunged at him, and then the two of them were fighting and Maureen was screaming at them to stop. The fight lasted only briefly, until one of Frederik's fists cracked against Augie's jaw and flung him reeling backward.

Augie doubled over and vomited until dry heaves racked him. Then with thick, half-formed words he ordered Maureen to get her things.

Frederik wondered if he'd broken Augie's jaw.

Maureen, sounding fearful, said, "Augie, I don't want to go to the mine. Pa's going to be..." She got a towel, and while she cleaned her brother's face, she kept pleading. "Augie, please?"

"What you say...between you and Pa," Augie finally told her. "We'll wait till morning, but you're going. And you get *him* out now."

Maureen rinsed the towel in a basin and hung it to dry before turning to Frederik. Her eyes asked a question.

*She wants me to decide for her,* Frederik thought, suddenly frightened in a way he hadn't been in those moments he'd fought with Augie. *If I want her to, Maureen will walk out of here with me now; will do what I tell her to do.*

"Maureen," he said awkwardly, "we're not... I'm not..."

Her voice didn't waver when she said, "Then thank you for a lovely day. I apologize for its ending."

Frederik moved through the evening chores hardly seeing the work he did. He wasn't ready to be responsible for someone else, and Maureen shouldn't expect him to be.

Uncle Joe had gone to a meeting in the lower valley, or Frederik might have asked him what to do. As it was, he couldn't decide, couldn't even settle on exactly what the choices were. He brought in stove wood, mended a piece of harness, and looked around for another job: anything to keep his mind off matters he couldn't help.

He picked up his violin, or fiddle, as Maureen called it, and then abruptly put it back down. He climbed the loft ladder. Come morning, he'd ask his uncle for advice.

But he couldn't sleep, not with his mind circling around the same questions: *What should I have done? Brought Maureen back here? To do what? Be what?*

He was still awake when the cabin door opened

around midnight. Frederik was surprised to hear voices, until he realized it was just his uncle talking with a neighbor.

He raised his head from his pillow so he could hear better.

"I'm giving up," Uncle Joe said. "The others can keep fighting if they want to, but I'm done with lawyers and with throwing good money after bad."

"So will you try to rebuy this place?"

"No, by *Gott,* that is *not* what I'll do. Why didn't anybody say, I'd like to know, that the railroad had already been granted this land, back before the Middlers started working it? Or when they sold it to me? They thought they had a legal right, and I believed they did. So, no, by *Gott,* I won't pay for my own land again *or* wait to be evicted."

"But if the Middlers were squatters..."

"No!"

Frederik had heard all this before but never heard it said with such finality. When the neighbor left, he untangled himself from the bedcovers and climbed down the ladder. "What's happened?"

"Just another lawyer's letter, but I've had enough. I'm going to pull out while I've still a bit of money to get a new place with a solid title."

"Where?" Frederik asked, his mind running over the homesteads up and down the Rattlesnake.

"There's good land at cheap prices in the Bitterroot, and the river there keeps the climate good. An apple orchard, I'm thinking."

"But..."

"We'll plant trees." Suddenly Uncle Joe looked weary and old. "We'll talk in the morning, nephew, but I've made up my mind. I aim to move within the month. Sooner, if I can."

Leaving his uncle sitting at the kitchen table, Frederik returned to the loft. Sometime later, he awoke with his heart thudding and his insides feeling sick with shame. *Maureen trusted me, and I failed her. I got her in trouble and then left her to face the consequences alone.*

No matter what tale Augie would or wouldn't volunteer, Naill O'Leary would see Augie's banged-up face and demand to know what had happened. He would be furious when he learned that Frederik had been with Maureen in the O'Leary cabin, and Frederik didn't even want to think how Naill might take it out on her.

With no clear plan in mind—just a conviction he had to try to help Maureen—at first light Frederik saddled Patch. He hurried to the O'Leary place on Rattlesnake Creek, only to find it already deserted. Looking through the cabin's single front window, he could see that Maureen and Augie had taken some of the cabin's meager furnishings. They'd left the table with the tablecloth still on it, but the candleholder Maureen had made was gone.

*Maybe Maureen thinks she's going to have to live up at*

*the mine,* Frederik thought. *Or I guess in that shack she said they have just below it.*

"Come on, Patch," he said, urging his horse into a fast trot.

When Frederik got to the gulch the O'Learys had taken over, he scanned the hillsides until he spotted a pile of raw earth high up. He marked the spot by a large rock outcropping a short distance away, and then he hurried along the gulch bottom, taking a trail that followed a small stream.

A blast of dynamite karoomed out, making Patch shy and balk.

"It's okay, Patch. Okay there," Frederik said. *If Naill and Augie are doing mining work already, things must be all right,* he told himself. *I'm going to find Maureen doing chores, cooking breakfast maybe.*

At last he reached a tiny, makeshift shack built directly on dirt. Augie O'Leary's big roan and Maureen's and Naill O'Leary's riding horses skittered nervously inside a barbed-wire pen. Frederik slipped off Patch and tied him to a tree.

"Maureen?" he called.

No one answered, and when Frederik opened the door, he didn't see anything but a couple of straight chairs, messy pallets, and an old stove.

Another *karoom* echoed through the gulch. *They must* all *be up there,* Frederik thought. He located the rock outcropping and angled up the hillside toward it until he came on a pack trail. Moving quickly along it, he glimpsed the earth pile ahead, and then, suddenly, he was standing on a narrow shelf of land almost completely taken up by a pit with the timbered entrance to a mine tunnel at its bottom.

The first person Frederik saw was Naill O'Leary, looking up from the floor of the pit. Shouting in an unintelligible bellow of rage, Naill started up a ladder.

Then Frederik saw Maureen backed against the hill on one side, her face battered. Sounding frantic, she called, "Frederik, go away!"

Augie appeared from the brush on Frederik's other side, veered away, and pushed past a loaded packhorse. He bumped against the animal, and a blanket-wrapped bundle fell off and broke open. Items tumbled across the ground.

"Augie, I just want to talk," Frederik called, starting after him. He turned back and looked toward the pit. "Mr. O'Leary!" he called. "I want to talk."

Naill, his face appearing at the edge of the pit, shouted something Frederik couldn't understand.

Maureen yelled, "Watch out! Frederik...Augie, no!"

Frederik spun and saw Augie leaning around the packhorse, aiming a rifle. Frederik dived for the ground as Augie fired. Maureen began screaming, and Frederik, rolling in a desperate effort to reach cover, saw Augie's expression turn to horror.

"Pa!" Maureen ran to the edge of the pit as Augie turned and began running down the hillside. She cried out, "No!"

Frederik, hurrying to her, saw Naill O'Leary lying at the pit's bottom, all blood where one eye should have been. *Augie's shot his own Pa,* Frederik thought, hardly able to take it in. *He was aiming at me but I moved ... and his bullet hit Naill.*

LATE THAT AFTERNOON, Uncle Joe and Frederik helped a sheriff's deputy load Naill O'Leary's body onto a horse. Then they again offered awkward words of comfort to Maureen, who was holding herself in stiff control.

Frederik struggled to grasp all the problems facing her. Bad as Maureen's father and brother had been, they had taken care of her. But with Naill dead and Augie run off, maybe soon to be arrested for causing Naill's death— the sheriff's deputy hadn't been much interested in taking it as an accident—what would Maureen do now?

Even if her father had left a good title to the O'Leary place on the creek, which he hadn't, she couldn't live on it by herself. Not anymore than she could live in the shack down in the gulch.

"Do you know what you'll do?" Frederik asked her.

"Go to my aunt's in town, if she'll have me."

"Of course she will," Uncle Joe said, appearing relieved. "And we'll see you're settled in before we leave."

At her questioning look, he explained, "Frederik and I are moving to the Bitterroot Valley. I'd already decided that, and after this violence today, I'm all the more ready to be done with the Rattlesnake."

"I'm not!" Frederik heard himself say. He wanted to live in these mountains the rest of his life. And he didn't want to go anyplace too far from Maureen. Still, he had a hard time not sounding scared when he said, "I guess I'll stay here. Maybe move up to the line dugout and do some trapping come winter."

Uncle Joe let out his breath in a little puff of frustration.

Frederik promised Maureen. "I'll get in to town to see you when I can."

"Please," she said, and her face kind of crumpled in. She bent down to pick up something from among the items that had fallen off the packhorse. Frederik recognized the punched can candleholder as she flung it away.

"Why'd you do that?" Frederik asked.

She answered, "I don't want the reminder. If I hadn't made it ... hadn't wanted to show you ..."

He thought, *It wasn't a candleholder that brought us here.*

F rederik, arriving in town for the first time since Christmas, looked forward to seeing Maureen. He hoped her aunt would invite him to have dinner with them in their small, rented house. She had the last time, and she'd even thawed enough to make Frederik feel welcome.

First, however, he had to sell the bundle of pelts he'd brought with him.

At the hide and fur exchange he watched a purchasing clerk count over $112.50 for furs from a dozen ermines, eight marten, three mink, two bobcats, and two beavers. A winter's worth of catching and skinning animals and then fleshing, stretching, and drying their pelts.

The earnings were a disappointment, although he'd probably done well considering the late start he'd gotten on the trapping season. Snow had blocked Patch out of the high country before Frederik could finish hauling supplies to his line huts, and that meant that by January he was using precious time to snowshoe down to valley cabins where he could trade pelts for as much food as he could carry.

And it hadn't helped that a few weeks ago, back in February, a wolverine had run his line, chewing up a half dozen animals before Frederik got to them. Still, to come out with just $112.50! And he'd have to use some of that to pay the people who'd boarded Patch for five months.

As he walked along residential streets on his way to Maureen's, he calculated his needs and how much he might make hiring out as a ranch hand come spring. He'd be glad to take that kind of work as long as he could get on someplace close. He'd live in a bunkhouse, be fed with the other hands, and put away every penny he made. And if he could get on with a logging outfit next winter and save those wages, then, maybe...

ALTHOUGH THE weather was freezing, Maureen came running out to meet him. He knew, even before he saw her expression, that something was wrong. Behind her, her aunt's house had a FOR LET sign on the door, and the windows were bare of curtains.

"What's going on?" Frederik asked.

"She's leaving," Maureen said. "Because of Augie. He's in jail, and..." Maureen broke off. "I'm sorry," she said, straightening her body into proud, straight lines. "This isn't the way to explain things."

"Let's get your coat," Frederik said. "We can go down to the park and talk."

Not until they were settled on a bench brushed clear of snow did he say, "Now. Start with Augie. He got picked up?"

"Just after New Year," Maureen answered. "And now he's been tried and found guilty of manslaughter. I guess the jury thought that even if his killing Pa was an accident, it happened because he was aiming the gun at you."

Frederik nodded. That was in the statements he and Maureen had given the sheriff's deputy.

"The newspaper reported the trial," Maureen said, "and that's why my aunt's moving to Seattle, where her daughter lives. She says she can't ever again hold her head up here."

A leaden feeling spread through Frederik. "Are you going with her?"

"No. I'm not invited. My aunt says she's sorry but she's had enough of the O'Leary family, with my pa driving off her sister and now Augie a criminal. She said she won't take bad blood to her daughter's."

Maureen looked away. "Anyway," she said, "I wouldn't leave here."

"Do you know what you'll do?" Frederik asked. In his mind, the question sounded like the echo that it was. He'd asked the same thing back in September.

Maureen answered, "I'll have to find work. Rent a room someplace."

*What kind of work?* Frederik wondered. There were few enough jobs for women, and Maureen, sixteen years old, with no high school diploma.... And if her own aunt didn't want an O'Leary around, maybe others wouldn't, either.

THREE DAYS LATER, he and Maureen stood in an unheated church and were married by a priest. All through the hurried service, the cleric looked at them with angry pity, seeming provoked that he had no better choices to offer.

Then, with Maureen behind Frederik on Patch and with her horse laden with food supplies, they rode across the bridge over Rattlesnake Creek and then north past the boarded-up house that no longer belonged to Uncle Joe.

They went by the abandoned O'Leary place on the creek. The door hung open, and snow lay in mounds inside.

They passed trails into the high country where Frederik had wintered, but a trapline dugout wasn't a place for a bride.

They went to the only place they could think of, to the shack below the O'Leary mine. As far as they knew, no one had laid claim to the land along the gulch bottom and certainly no one else would want that old shack.

When they pulled up in front, the depressing place was already in deep shadow. Frederik kicked through a snowdrift, pushed the door open, and stepped back. The inside stank of animals: mice and probably something bigger, maybe whatever had knocked the stovepipe loose and scattered soot. The few household goods had been chewed to tags of litter, and rodent droppings were everywhere.

Frederik quickly closed the door before Maureen could see.

"You know," he said, "a ways back I noticed a spruce with a clear space under it the size of a room. I wonder if Mrs. Bottner would like to spend her wedding night camping out?"

Tomorrow would be time enough to face what they'd come to.

# TESSIE

On my first morning at my new academic school—earlier in September than my music school would start—I stood before a bulletin board and tried to get my bearings. All around me kids who hadn't seen one another since June were trying to cram a summer's talk into the few minutes before classes began. The school was only for professional kids and kids working toward careers in the performing arts, and it went from the upper middle grades through senior high, so the voices around me ranged in pitch from little-kid thin to almost grown-up.

I'd hoped the bulletin board would have a map of the school's layout, but instead I found tacked-up notices of concert programs and playbills from shows where students had parts. *Wow,* I thought, spotting one from a new hit musical. A cast member's name was highlighted in yellow. *Someone from this school is in that?*

A teacher called, "Time to get to your rooms, everybody," and I turned just as a boy came up to me.

"I've been watching for you," he said as I recognized the cello player who'd wished me good luck with my music school audition. "I wondered if you'd be one of the new wunderkind here."

I started to draw back and then realized he wasn't hassling me. He was teasing, sure, but he was also welcoming me to a place where special talent was what everyone had. At that instant, I understood I was at last in a school where I belonged. It was an idea so overwhelming that it made tears fill my eyes and spill over.

"Hey, don't cry!" he said. "I didn't mean anything bad." He fumbled in a sweatshirt pocket and pulled out a cloth that had been used for cleaning rosin dust. "Here. Blow your nose on this."

I found out that his name was Ben and that he was an eighth grader like me.

BEN TOOK CHARGE of me those first weeks, kind of the way a nice big brother might take care of a little sister.

He made sure that I met everybody—dancers and actors and singers, as well as other kids who wanted to be classical musicians. I got to know a girl who played world-class chess and a boy who played pro golf.

My school seemed to me to be the most extraordinary place, filled with kids leading double lives. Individually we each had our commitment: an instrument to practice or ballet routines to learn; a music or dance school to attend or a coach to work with. But here, although we carried our commitment with us—identified ourselves by our art—here we went to math classes and wrote book reports and gossiped in the school cafeteria just like kids did in schools everywhere.

At first it surprised me how teachers worked around whatever came up. When I heard my science teacher reviewing material for a kid who'd have to miss class during rehearsals for a new show, I remembered Ms. Watkins, my sixth grade teacher who hadn't wanted me returning from lunch late because of my violin lessons.

And I could just imagine what she'd have to say about theater kids regularly taking off Wednesday afternoons to perform in matinees.

Sometimes kids would even disappear for weeks at a time, like when the golfer went on tour. Or the models. This girl who was really, really stunning was forever taking off to do fashion shoots in places like Frankfurt and Tahiti. Mostly the kids didn't make a big deal about it, and our teachers didn't, either. In fact, they went out of their way to help everybody keep up.

I heard one of them explaining it to the parents of another new student. "When you consider how stressful adolescence is anyway, and then you layer on all the responsibilities these kids carry, it makes you wonder how they handle things as well as they do," he said. "Sometimes I think our most important job is giving them some space."

I got to know a couple of dancers best, Kiah and

Eleni, who went to ballet school on Saturdays the way I went to music school. And sometimes I hung around with two other dancers, both named Amy.

And there was Ben, of course. After a while he stopped treating me like a little sister. We didn't exactly become boyfriend and girlfriend that year, but we didn't exactly *not,* either.

That year zoomed by, and soon I was into another, and I thought I must be the happiest freshman in all New York. I still loved my academic school, and Saturdays...

On Saturdays I'd set my alarm for 5:00 A.M. so I could get in my practice time and still leave early for music school. I wanted to be the first to arrive so that I wouldn't miss anything, not even one minute of being together with the friends I had there. I'd wait on the nearby plaza knowing somebody would call, "Hey, Tess!" and come over.

Pretty soon there'd be a small group of us laughing and gossiping. Early-morning tourists would stare at us, because of the instruments we all carried, and their curiosity made me feel special instead of odd.

Other than Ben, my music school friends weren't the same kids I hung around with in regular school. I didn't know them as well, because some of us only saw each other on Saturdays, but we understood one another better. We were all musicians who wanted our music to be great, and that's what our Saturdays were all about.

We took theory classes where we learned how to talk about music and analyze it. In classes called solfège we worked on training our ears—perfecting our pitch and rhythm skills and learning to recognize musical elements when we heard them. And we all participated in an orchestra. That was my favorite part of Saturdays, when my violin and everybody else's instruments all blended together to make music that soared.

Not that it always soared. Sometimes our conductor spent more time tapping his baton on his music stand— "Hold it! Stop playing, people. Something's wrong"— than he did actually conducting us. And even though working out a problem was interesting, nobody wanted to be responsible for whatever mistake he'd heard.

I made my share of errors, but from my seat in the second row of violins, I could see straight across to Ben in the front row of cellos, and he always knew when I needed a smile.

Besides, I could hear that my playing was getting better and better, gaining a polish it had never had before.

And then there were Sundays, with matinee concerts and operas and an occasional ballet to go to, and I had friends to go with. We didn't go every week, because we didn't always have time and because even with standing-room tickets bought with student discounts, performances still cost a lot. But we went as often as we could.

At first Mom worried. "I don't like you out on your own in the city," she said. "I want you safe. And shouldn't you be practicing or doing homework?"

"Mom, nothing's going to happen to me on a Sunday afternoon in a busy, safe part of town," I told her. "Besides, I'll get graded down if I *don't* go. My teachers practically assigned us to go hear this violist from Russia who's never played in this country before, and—"

"And I don't like your going by yourself."

"I'm not. I'm meeting a half-dozen kids."

A frown furrowed Mom's forehead. "From your academic school or your music school?"

"Some of both."

"Boys or girls?"

"Both."

"I don't want you running around like some teenager without purpose."

"Mom, I'm going to a concert!"

She shook her head, but she also gave me ticket money. "Just don't get any wrong ideas about who's making the rules around here," she said. "You're a long way from knowing what's best for you."

MOST PEOPLE don't buy standing-room tickets by choice, but I did. I always felt special taking up a position among really dedicated music lovers, which standing-room-only patrons pretty much had to be. Usually Ben and I stood next to each other.

After a performance a bunch of us would head to a coffee shop where we'd crowd around a corner table in the back, ordering the least we could without being thrown out. Then we'd dissect the afternoon's performance into the tiniest bits.

We had opinions on everything from a conductor's timing to the volume of a timpani section, and we all tried to tell them at once. We commented on the choice of music and gossiped about composers—dead and alive—as though they were personal acquaintances.

Sometimes Ben would catch my eye and give me a private smile. Sometimes, if we were sitting side by side, he'd give my hand a quick squeeze. And sometimes we'd keep on holding hands.

I'd leave the coffee shop wishing the afternoon could have stretched on and on.

When Dad would call later on—he always called Sunday evenings—I'd try to tell him how happy I was. "School's so good—both my schools—and you'd like my friends. They're all so talented, and we talk and talk..."

"So New York's going okay, huh?" he'd say, and I could hear that he was glad for me and also a little sad.

I always told him, "You can come visit. I'll take you to meet everybody."

"Maybe one day," he'd say, although we both knew he probably wouldn't. Somehow, gradually, Mom's and my living apart from him had become Mom's and his separation, and the separation, once in lawyers' hands, had become a divorce.

I'd have felt really bad for my parents except neither one seemed unhappy about *being* divorced. In fact, it all seemed to have happened with so little regret that I wondered if they might not have been glad the move to New York got things rolling.

Except, of course, I knew Dad missed seeing me grow up.

Midway through November Dad and I were having one of our Sunday night conversations when he said, "Don't get too busy to come home."

"I won't," I said. "But, Dad, everything is so great here. I like school, and I've got friends—Kiah, Eleni, Ben..."

"Ben? A friend or a boyfriend?"

"Well..."

"Use good judgment. Hold him up to the questions I'd ask if I was there." Dad's voice dropped into a deeper imitation of itself. "Where are you taking my daughter? What time will you have her home? Who's driving?"

"Dad, nobody *drives* in New York. You've got to be practically a senior citizen to get a license."

"You know what I mean. And, Tess, about your violin...I'll come hear you play one day. Meanwhile, remember your old man's rooting for you."

———

I HAD SOMEBODY else rooting for me now, too, and that was Mr. Stubner, the violin teacher I'd started with when I began music school. At first I was a little afraid of him, because other kids told stories about how he lost patience with students and even dropped them when they didn't meet his expectations.

Also, I'd never had a violin teacher who was so reserved—almost formal—or who had such planned-out requirements for what I was to master. I loved some of the new music he introduced me to, but he also made me learn some that I didn't care for at all.

I struggled with pages of violin exercises where black notes ran so close together that they looked like bands of charcoal. And instead of exaggerating dynamics to cover where my technique was weak, I had to dig into problems head-on.

He wrapped it all up in a ball he called discipline, and I gradually learned that he didn't mean how much I practiced, but how—and what—I worked on. He wanted me to command a full range of fundamentals that would let me take my violin playing as far as possible.

I worked for what I could learn, and I worked for his rare, pleased nod of approval.

Ben and I talked about everything. I told him, "I know that one day my violin playing's got to turn into a job, but I wish it didn't have to. I wish I could keep going to school forever."

He said, "I thought you wanted to be a concert soloist."

"I'd like to play well enough to be one, but to actually have that kind of career... It's scary to even think about. Although I suppose I'll have to try. Mom brought me to New York so I'll have a chance."

"You're here for your mom?"

"I didn't say that. Anyway, what about you?" I asked. "What do you want?"

"Too much," Ben answered, with a quick shake of his head. "I came here for my cello, but since I started studying composing, I've begun thinking that's the direction I want to go. I feel bad about it, because of all that my folks have sacrificed to help me become a cellist."

"Have you told them?"

"I did the last time I was home. They're worried about me getting into such an uncertain field, but they accept that it's a decision I have to make for myself."

I gave him a wry smile. "Mom and I aren't there yet," I said. "Actually, I doubt if she ever will be."

COME SPRING, Ben and I began taking an occasional afternoon off from school. We weren't supposed to, of course, but it was as close as we could get to going out.

None of my friends dated. We didn't have time.

Anyway, sometimes Ben would catch me in the hall at our academic school—or I'd go find him. Then whoever it was would ask, "You got anything you can't miss this afternoon?" That was our code for "You want to cut classes?" We only did it once in a while. Any more and our teachers would have asked for notes confirming the special music practices that we gave as our excuses to be absent.

The most difficult thing about those afternoons off was deciding where to go. New York held so much that choosing one thing meant not choosing a hundred others.

The first time we took off, we caught a bus to Times Square and hung around there. We spent another afternoon riding the subways, getting off to explore Greenwich Village and Tribeca. Ben tried to write that day into a piece of music he called "Cityscape," using weird instruments and jangling, thumping rhythms to represent shops and street vendors and noisy, rushing crowds. He got a B on it and the instructor wrote, "Interesting effort but a bit hard on the ears."

One time we went to the top of the Empire State Building, and on another day we walked across the Brooklyn Bridge and back.

"I never want to leave this city," I told him.

"Don't you ever miss Montana?"

"If I think about it, I do. But there's not much here to remind me of it." I gestured toward a plywood wall shielding a construction site on one side of the street and then at a glass-fronted skyscraper opposite. "Ben, when was the last time you touched a tree?"

"Touched a tree? You mean like hug-a-tree environmental?"

"No! I mean like felt bark. Smelled leaves."

Forty-five minutes later we sat in Central Park, our backs against a maple, and I tried to describe a mountain forest that stretched as far as a person could see. I told Ben about how a forest viewed from a distance might look all the same, but when you got in it, you'd find more kinds of trees and flowers and grasses than you could imagine, and more kinds of shrubs and brambles. You'd walk among Douglas firs and larches, spruces and ponderosa pines, and each species would have a different kind of bark.

"It sounds to me like you're missing Montana right now," he said.

"A little. I'd like you to see it."

The only thing wrong with that afternoon was the let-down I felt when we said good-bye and caught our separate buses home.

One day early in our sophomore year, we got the afternoon off without even having to cut class. It happened when smoke from a nearby restaurant fire filled our school and everyone was dismissed until the building could be aired out. Delighted with the unexpected freedom, a bunch of us headed to a fast-food place.

Besides Ben and me, Kiah and Eleni were there. Also a voice student named Katya, who I didn't know very well, and two more guys: a French-horn player named Chi; and Liam, an acting student who had a part in a Broadway show. Liam had a grin that made you grin back, and while he used to be just cute, lately he'd become downright handsome. *Audiences,* I thought, *must love him.*

I was offering around a plate of onion rings when my gaze fell on a newspaper that someone had left on the next table. "Hey," I said to Liam. "This is Wednesday. Don't you have a matinee?"

"Not today."

"How come? Is this your alternate's day?" Shows with kid actors often let them share roles so the kids wouldn't have to work eight performances a week.

Liam shook his head. I thought he wasn't going to explain, but then he burst out, "I got fired."

"But why?" Kiah asked. "You're a great actor."

"I outgrew my costume. My own fault for having a summer growth spurt." Liam was trying to joke, but he sounded bitter. "It's cheaper for a show to replace an actor than to have a new costume made."

"That's awful," I said.

"It happens to more than just actors," Katya said. "The biggest fight my mom and I ever had was over a wedding job I didn't get because the bride hired a curly-haired little eight-year-old instead. Mom said I must not have sung my best, and I told her the reason I didn't get hired was I had braces on my teeth and my forehead was breaking out and I had boobs. The stupid bride didn't want boobs. She wanted cute!"

I glanced at Ben. He was looking down, picking at his hamburger bun like it was the most fascinating thing he'd ever seen.

"So what did your mom say?" Eleni asked.

"That she'd make me an appointment with a dermatologist." Katya laughed, but her eyes welled. "I guess I ought to be grateful she didn't make me wear a girdle around my chest!"

"MOM," I SAID that evening, "do you think Mr. Capianelli and the others—all the people who went to my recital—would they have liked my violin playing so much if I'd been older?"

"What?" Mom asked, her mind someplace else. "Oh. Of course they would have, Tessie, although you might not have gotten the same attention."

I wondered, *Is that a yes or a no? What if I'd played my recital at nineteen instead of nine? What if I'd just been Mr. Capianelli's student Tess, instead of his precocious Tess?*

I couldn't get Katya out of my mind. I'd never tell Katya, of course, but I'd heard her sing, and I didn't think she was all that good. Maybe she'd needed to be a sweet little girl to get as far as she had.

When I got ready for bed I spent a long time looking into the bathroom mirror. I told myself that I ought to be pleased with what I saw. That I was lucky my eyes looked good even without makeup. That I ought to be glad my face was showing cheekbones and my body finally getting some shape.

Of course I didn't want to be little again, but I did feel like someone had played an unfair trick on me. And while I told myself it wasn't what I looked like but how well I played my violin that mattered most, Liam and Katya had put a doubt in me I hadn't had before.

"Tessie," Mom said, tapping on the door. "You need to turn your light off."

"Mom!" I said, snapping even though she wasn't the one who'd made me mad. "I'm old enough to know how much sleep I need. And stop calling me Tessie. It doesn't fit anymore."

# TESS

In the late afternoon a distant bank of dark clouds gives us our first hint we're going to lose our good camping weather. By early evening the sky is heavily overcast, the temperature is dropping rapidly, and we're feeling a few drops of rain. We eat dinner quickly, and I help Dad wrap the food bag in plastic and hoist it out of reach of animals.

Then, chilly and with nothing left to do, we all retreat to our sleeping bags.

I try to read but don't have enough light to see decently, and as soon as I put my book down, Amy says, "Tell me about Ben."

"You've got his picture, so you know what he looks like."

"But what's *he* like?"

"Well, he's my age. Really nice. Really talented. Really busy."

"He looks Chinese in his picture."

"Vietnamese, or half, anyway. That's what his mom is."

Amy thinks about that. "Have you met her?"

"Just once, when Ben's folks traveled to New York to hear him play. They can't afford to live there and also pay for his school and music."

"Then who does Ben live with?"

"Officially he stays with a cousin, but he lives with some other guys."

Amy's eyes widen. "With *nobody* to be the boss of him?"

"Nobody." I throw her a sideways glance. "He's got just himself to see he gets his schoolwork and practicing done, plus laundry and cooking and rounding up paying gigs."

"Oh," Amy says, sounding more impressed and less envious. "I don't think I'd like that."

"Me, either," I tell her.

Then my face gets warm as I consider how my leaving New York the way I did might seem to someone who has to work so hard to be there. Probably Ben wouldn't think I'm ungrateful, but somebody else might.

Amy says, "Mom and I were on our own when she went back to school."

"Where was your dad?"

"He was gone and we didn't need him. Anyway, Pop says I'm *his* girl now."

Amy turns to face me, propping herself up on one

elbow, and in a suddenly worried voice she asks, "Do you mind?"

"No," I answer, realizing that I really don't.

"Good," she says, lying back down again. "We're pillow talking, aren't we?"

"I guess, if you can call rolled-up sweatshirts pillows."

"Like at a sleepover."

"I guess," I repeat. "I've never been to one."

"Why not?"

"There wasn't time. Not with academic school on weekdays and music school on Saturdays and then homework and practicing."

"Whoa!" Amy says. "You went to school on *Saturday*? You went to *two* schools? I wouldn't. Nobody could make me. It's probably against the law. Did you tell your mom that?"

"It's against the law *not* to go to school, not the other way around," I tell her.

"But..." Amy twists her fingers, crossing one over another. "Didn't you ever have time for fun?"

"Maybe not the kind of fun you're thinking of, but, yes. A lot."

"I don't see how. Why didn't you just quit your violin? I mean, a long time ago?"

"Because I love playing it."

I want to explain more, but I doubt she'd understand. Anyway, I wouldn't know how to tell her what it's like to wake up in the morning hardly able to wait to take your violin from its case because the few hours that you were sleeping were a long time not to have it in your hands.

And how could I explain about Saturdays and music school? About how included—almost *embraced*—you can feel in the moments before orchestra practice begins, when you're tuning and warming up, and all around you other musicians are doing the same thing.

Some days you hold your breath watching for the baton downstroke that will set a hundred instruments playing together. You don't want to be an instant late plunging in; don't want to miss an instant of being carried along on sound that comes from every side and up from your violin, along your jawbone, to your ear.

When you go home at the dark end of a winter afternoon, after you've gone to music classes and ensemble and orchestra and maybe had a private lesson, you're so keyed-up weary you can hardly eat your dinner.

And then there's still more practicing to do. And tired as you are, you get on it, because maybe this night will be one of the special ones. A night when your violin comes to life in your hands and everything you play comes out better and better. When the music flies and you fly with it, higher and better and faster until you're playing more beautifully than you ever have.

A night like that, you want to keep going forever.

That's what I want to explain to Amy. But her sputtering breath makes me think she's gone to sleep, and so I don't struggle to find words for what I could say more easily with my violin. Instead, I repeat to myself, "Because I love it."

"Tess?" Amy says, tugging on my sleeping bag. Rain is drumming loudly on the tent. "Are you awake?"

"I wasn't before," I tell her. "I am now."

"I need to go to the bathroom."

"Wait a bit," I tell her. "Maybe the storm will let up."

She says, "I don't think I can."

"It's up to you." I'm glad it's her and not me who needs to go out.

"Will you take me?"

"Oh, for . . ." Going out in such weather is the last thing I want to do, except for feeling as guilty as I will if I refuse. "Okay. Yes."

THE NEXT TIME I wake up, the tent is dim and the downpour continues with the steady, hard beat of a rain likely to last a long time. I squint at my watch and am surprised to see it's after eight o'clock. I don't hear Dad or Meg up, and Amy is a long lump in her sleeping bag. I burrow deeper into my own, glad no one's rushing to get out in the bad weather. I wonder if I actually heard thunder through the night or just imagined it. Either way, it was part of dreams I'd like to return to.

Dreams of thunder and furious music and words printed above notes. Summertime. *Turbulent summertime.*

I realize I must have been dreaming about Vivaldi's Summer Concerto that I played in Germany—or tried to play. There's a section where the rhythm switches to a torrent of headlong sixteenth notes, and the words above the music staff say there's a thunderstorm going on.

*The storm splits the sky...* Those words belong to a poem that's been included with the music since the concerto was first published back in the 1800s. People think Vivaldi probably wrote it himself.

I can hear the count of the music, the accent on the first note of each measure. It has a driving rhythm of four lightning-fast one-a-and-a notes for each beat, pounded into three-quarter time... *One,* two, three. *One,* two, three. *One,* two, three. *One,* two, three... like hard, steady rain.

Drowsily, I try to pick out the same pattern in the rain pounding down on the tent, but I can't make it work. Still, I think if I could choose music just right for this morning, the Vivaldi concerto would be it.

I'd like some music right now. I'd just stay in my sleeping bag and listen.

We eat breakfast hunkered under the tents' rain flies. It's a miserable affair, cups of oatmeal and hot drinks that we hold in gloved hands.

I wear every bit of clothing I have with me—long pants and two shirts under my sweatshirt under my rain jacket.

Dad, looking like a dark green bat in a flapping poncho that covers him head to shins, asks, "What do you think? Push on or wait it out?"

Nobody argues when Meg answers, "Let's hole up a few hours."

We spend the morning in shifting combinations of people playing cards and napping and reading. The rain gets harder, if anything, and lunch is another miserable, wet affair because Dad won't let us take food inside the tents.

"I won't spill anything," Amy protests, but Meg backs up Dad.

"And if you did," Meg says, "the scent would linger on as an invitation to wild animals. You want to get visited by a skunk?"

"Yes!" Amy says. "I'd tell him to spray you and Pop and Tess!"

When we finish eating, Meg disappears into her and Dad's tent, and the rest of us start a marathon game of hearts. Every so often, Dad steps outside to look for lighter skies, but each time he comes back shaking his head. We play until Amy, after a couple of disastrous hands, starts hiding the queen of spades.

"Maybe, rain or not, you and I ought to go for a walk," Dad tells her. "Tess, want to come?"

"I think I'll go see what Meg's doing," I say.

SHE'S WRITING in a notebook, and her Rattlesnake folder is open on her lap.

"Hi," she says, looking up. "Who won?"

"I'm not sure. Amy was keeping score and got the columns mixed up. What are you working on?"

"Catching up my journal, or trying to. I keep thinking about Katharina Bottner and wondering what her family's story was. And where they fit into the overall scheme of things." She gestures toward a folded sleeping bag. "Come in. Sit down."

"I won't be bothering you?"

"I'll be glad for your company."

Leaving my boots at the tent entrance, I make myself

comfortable while she continues to stare at her notebook with a little frown creasing her forehead.

"Meg, why do you care so much?" I ask. "About things that happened so long ago?"

She takes time choosing her words. "You're really asking why I'm an archaeologist, aren't you? I suppose because I'm fascinated by the mysteries that the past holds. And I believe our own time will be better if we understand how people have lived across history."

Then she says, "I could ask you the same question. Why do you care about music? Or for that matter, why does anyone become passionate about a particular thing?"

Her questions are the kind that my friends and I used to discuss in our coffee-shop gatherings. But that was us kids, and that we *were* passionate about our art was a given.

Now I tell Meg, "I don't know. I used to say I couldn't live without my violin, even though I knew I really could. I mean, lots of people don't play instruments, and if I'd never played one then I couldn't miss it. You can't miss what you don't know, can you?"

"I think you might feel something was lacking."

"I suppose."

Meg hands me the Rattlesnake folder. "You're welcome to read through this if you want. It's got everything I could find on the Bottners and their homesite, as well as an assortment of other odds and ends."

While Meg writes in her journal, I scan through photocopies of legal documents and then slow to read a newspaper story about a government land survey. Apparently the survey results started a dispute between a railroad company and some Rattlesnake residents.

I go back to the beginning of the article and read more carefully, but the reporter doesn't provide much background, and his old-fashioned writing style makes it hard to understand the little bit he does give.

Meg, noticing what I'm looking at, says, "I puzzled over that, also, wondering if Katharina's family was involved, but I think the legal hassles were mostly resolved before Frederik Bottner filed his land claim. It's more likely that the earlier Bottner—Johann Bottner—would have been caught up in that controversy."

Other newspaper stories deal with ongoing issues like wildfire danger and timber sales, and a pair of brief pieces tell of the shooting death of a miner named Naill O'Leary and the related subsequent arrest of his son.

I glance at a couple of maps and read a 1916 newspaper clipping about a dance where Frederik Bottner provided fiddle music, and then I turn to some photos. The first shows a small building that's apparently a schoolhouse. A woman in a long skirt, holding a large book, stands out in front of it, behind a row of seven children. "What do the letters and numbers on here mean?" I ask.

"They're an archive reference," Meg answers. "The identifier for the original photo."

The next picture has two labels in addition to its identifier. The first, printed in ink in the photocopy's margin, says, "Acquired 1956; source unknown." The other label is written in old-fashioned script across the picture itself. It says, "So lonely! Deserted cabin, Rattlesnake Valley, 1908."

"Was this Katharina's home?" I ask.

"No. The dates are wrong," Meg answers. "She wasn't born for another couple of years."

"Do you know whose place this was?"

"No. That particular cabin doesn't show up in any other Rattlesnake pictures I could find, so it might have been destroyed early on. Actually, I meant to leave that picture in my office along with some other material probably not relevant to the Bottners."

I continue to study the photo, which is a very nice shot of a very sorry looking place. A window—the only window on the whole front side—is broken. The cabin's door hangs by one hinge, and what appears to be a table is visible inside.

"It looks like somebody left here in a hurry," I say. "They left their things."

Meg says, "Doesn't it make you wonder why?"

Just then we hear Dad shouting, "Helloooo!"

A moment later Amy barges in. "You missed so much!" she says, shaking off water the way a wet dog does.

"Stop!" Meg and I exclaim in unison.

"We found this meadow with actual frogs," Amy says,

"and Pop says it's just the kind of place where deer go to eat early in the morning. Do you want to watch for them tomorrow, Tess?"

"I think we're going to leave when the rain lets up," I tell her.

"But if we're still here?"

Dad pops his head inside the tent. "Hey, kiddo!" he says to Amy. "I thought you and I were going to make hot chocolate." He tells Meg and me, "We're going to mix it with orange drink and some mint we found. And we'll share!"

"Orange drink?" Meg asks, looking dubious.

"Orange chocolate," he says firmly. "A Thaler specialty."

"Then I don't want to miss it," she says. "By the time you two get the stove cooking and the water hot, Tess and I will be along."

I CONTINUE LOOKING through the Rattlesnake folder, stopping at a 1906–1907 list of Missoula County High School students with the name Maureen O'Leary, a sophomore, highlighted. Behind it is a copy of a marriage certificate for Frederik Bottner and Maureen O'Leary dated March 14, 1908. "Are these Katharina's parents?" I ask.

Meg nods.

"But they're so young!"

"Maureen O'Leary certainly was," she says. "I don't

know Frederik Bottner's age, but she couldn't have been more than sixteen." She shakes her head. "You wonder why. Maybe it was related to the shooting."

"Maybe they were in love," I say.

"Maybe." Meg sounds unconvinced. "But sixteen is awfully young to make a decision that will affect the rest of your life."

I glance up quickly, but if Meg's referring to anything more than the Bottners' marriage, her face doesn't show it.

"Are you guys still talking?" Amy asks, ducking under the rain fly. "Come on! The chocolate's done, and I put in lemonade mix besides orange drink, and Pop says it's the most unusual hot chocolate he's ever tasted."

# FREDERIK
## 1909–1916

They lost two ewes to a cougar before Frederik tracked and shot it. It looked as if all of the new batch of lambs might live, though, even the ones born during a late, brief blizzard and taken inside to be warmed to life by the stove.

The lambs were children of the dozen orphan lambs Frederik and Maureen had started out with their first spring together. Frederik had gotten them in payment for three weeks of hard work, and Maureen had raised them on bottles.

Now, during the sleepless days and nights of lambing time, Frederik sometimes saw his thoughts reflected in his wife's eyes. *We've made it through one whole year.*

As Frederik moved through the cold chores of a March afternoon, he looked forward to the evening. He and Maureen were still living in the same shack, but now its walls were chinked and lined with newspaper and the outsides banked with straw and some lingering snow. It kept the wind out and the stove warmth in.

Maureen would have a good dinner waiting—maybe venison with brown gravy, along with the sourdough rolls he'd seen rising. When they were done eating, they'd talk awhile and then Maureen would ask him to get out his fiddle. He was getting pretty good on it, able to play almost any tune they could remember.

And then, later, they'd sleep safe together.

As THE LAMBS got older, they became comic to watch. One June day Frederik and Maureen, resting against the trunk of a tree they'd just felled, laughed at the small band of them jumping back and forth across the stream. The littlest lamb, afraid to jump, bleated piteously whenever the others went to the far side.

"They're going to wear themselves out," Maureen said.

"What else have they got to do? You think we can teach them to pull a saw?"

"It would be nice."

Between clearing land and planting a large garden, they were working every daylight hour. The garden was still soggy ground, but Frederik supposed that by midsummer they'd be hauling water to it, along with keeping up on everything else.

"Someday I'd like to put in a ditch to divert water from higher up," he said, thinking about the one he'd built with his uncle. "It would make things easier down here and also let us flood-irrigate some pasture."

Frederik, as legal head of household, had filed a homestead claim on the gulch. It had seemed a huge step to take, but now that he and Maureen were no longer squatters who might be driven off it, he was enjoying making plans for their place.

The lambs wheeled about and tore through the woods, toward the nearest hillside, and as Maureen's gaze followed, the expression on her face hardened.

In all the time they'd lived here, she'd not visited the mine once, and Frederik had gone up only long enough to board over its entrance and bring down what he thought they might use. One of these days he'd get around to cleaning up the junk Naill and Augie had scattered about, but right now there was too much else to do.

Besides, Maureen didn't like him anywhere near the mine. She called it a hateful, mean place.

It was August of another year, and the land under Frederik's hurrying feet was dry and hard, and dead grass crunched with his weight. That was the loudest sound, except for Maureen's and his hard breathing as they carried water from the stream to their parched garden.

It seemed hauling water was about all they'd done for weeks now, trying to keep things alive through the driest summer Frederik remembered. Even the old-timers said 1910 was turning out to be a drought year beyond their ken.

Back in the spring, when snowmelt had turned everything green, Frederik had made plans to build a barn with a big loft that would hold all the hay he expected to cut this summer. But then the spring rains that usually followed green-up didn't come, and after a while the stunted meadow grass stopped growing and turned brown.

Now the garden was their best hope for avoiding disaster. Dried, canned, or stored in the root cellar, its produce would feed them this winter. And anything extra could be sold, which would bring in money for buying hay, which might let them keep all their breeding ewes.

He emptied a bucket of water around a circle of pole beans and another on the squash bed and then turned to go back to the stream for more.

"I wish you'd stop," he told Maureen, as she passed him with two full buckets of her own. He worried about the baby she was carrying inside her. "Or at least slow down."

The next time they passed each other, he saw her stagger.

THEIR DAUGHTER was born hours later, three weeks early. Frederik delivered her, tending Maureen as gently as he could and praying that what he knew from birthing livestock would be enough.

They named her Katharina, for Frederik's mother. Maureen suggested it.

Katharina Maureen. Frederik insisted on that.

Once he was satisfied that Maureen and the baby were all right, Frederik returned to the garden, picked up the buckets, and resumed ferrying water.

Frederik, sitting up in the wagon where he'd spent the night, looked out at the dawn-lit school yard in the middle of Spring Gulch. The spring morning was cold, and a friend who was starting a breakfast fire saw him and called, "Hey, fiddle player, come give a hand making coffee."

Maureen reached out to check that Katharina, going on six years old now, was still asleep beside her. "Just a few minutes and then I'll get up," she told Frederik. "I want to think some more about last night's party." She smiled up at him. "I was so proud of you playing so everybody could dance."

"Stay there if you want to," he said, "but Mrs. Swenson's coming this way."

"Oh, so early!" Maureen said, but she sat up and pulled a quilt around her shoulders. "Good morning, Mrs. Swenson."

"Good morning, child," the older woman said. "I

came to say don't pass by my place without stopping. I've got the best rhubarb in the valley, and I want you to dig yourself a good start."

Maureen leaned down and gave her an impulsive hug. "Oh, I am so happy this morning. Have I told you that when we get home, Frederik and I are going to begin work on a second room for our house?"

Frederik couldn't help smiling at her pleasure. He'd long since turned their home into more cabin than shack, but up until now, it hadn't gotten any bigger.

"RIGHT HERE," Maureen said, using her toe to scrape a mark in the back corner of her garden. "Rhubarb's a long-lasting plant. I want this one growing where it won't be disturbed."

"Right," said Frederik, stabbing his shovel several inches from the mark to tease her. "How many pies is this going to buy me?"

"None this year. You're just going to have to work on promise."

They ate lunch after the rhubarb was in, and after that they pounded stakes where they wanted the corners of the new room to be. They'd decided to put it on the side of the cabin that needed fixing, anyway.

Maureen became briefly wistful. "Our place is so different now, I mostly forget it was ever Pa and Augie's mine shack. But now we're getting ready to fix it up more..."

Frederik tilted his head in what he hoped looked like understanding. He never had found the right thing to say about Naill O'Leary, and as for Augie—Frederik and Maureen had no idea what happened to him once he got out of jail. Maybe they never would.

As they forced a temporary support under a rotting foundation log, Frederik said, "I've been thinking that as long as we're repairing and building, maybe we ought to run a porch across the front."

"I'd love that," Maureen said. "Wide enough for a rocking chair and maybe a swing."

"Papa!" Katharina called from where she was leaning over a fence to pet Patch. "See? He won't hurt me. Please can I ride?"

"When you're older!" Frederik called back. "Next year, maybe!"

"You know," Maureen said, "I've been riding since before I can remember."

"Me, too," Frederik said. "But I don't want Katharina growing up as fast as we had to."

"She's almost six . . . And she's not asking to do something dangerous. She'll never learn to take care of herself if we don't start letting her try."

It was an ongoing argument. Frederik thought he understood Maureen's determination to see that their daughter learned to do everything she could as soon as possible. She didn't want Katharina ever to be left with as few choices as Maureen herself had had those first years Frederik had known her.

But Katharina was still such a little thing. Put her on a horse and next she'd be wanting to ride off somewhere, and who knew what dangers she'd get into. Frederik saw no need for taking risks with her as long as he could keep her safe.

"Come on, now!" he called. "Come look where we're going to put our new room."

THEY FINISHED the addition to the cabin a month later and celebrated with a Sunday afternoon picnic by the stream.

*A day couldn't be any better,* Frederik thought as he ate a second piece of chocolate cake. *Or the woods sound any nicer.*

*Or,* he thought, looking around, *a place be any prettier.* A red brown calf nursed at its mama. Their biggest crop of lambs yet were chasing each other about. The potato field was a skim of new green. The sour cherry trees Maureen had planted were trying to blossom.

His gaze traveled up the hillside to the irrigation system he'd finally finished—two miles of ditch dug and wood flume built. Diverting water from the stream's upper end to run along the high edge of their fields had been a huge job, but now he could open gates and flood anywhere he wanted.

His gaze sharpened as sparkling movement caught his eye. Frowning, he said to Maureen, "Does that look like water gushing out up there?"

Up on the hillside, he wondered what animal had used his flume for a step stool. Something big, he guessed, a bear or a mountain lion. Otherwise, the nails he'd used to anchor the wood trough to a tree trunk wouldn't have pulled clear out.

"Frederik!" Maureen called. "Is Katharina with you?"

"No!" *That child!* he thought. *What trick is she playing on her mother now? Probably hiding under the bed the way she did yesterday.* "Look in the cabin!"

He went back to repairing the flume but was interrupted by a sound like a shot. It surprised him—people didn't come into this gulch very often, and hunting season was over, anyway.

"Frederik, what was that?" Maureen called. *"Katharina!"*

Maureen hadn't found her?

Suddenly afraid, Frederik started up the hillside, hurrying toward where the sound had come from. His pace picked up even faster when he hit the overgrown old pack trail, and fear gripped him tighter and tighter. *Katharina can't be at the old mine. She can't be,* he told himself. *But a sound like a rifle shot doesn't just happen.*

Then he got a whiff of a sharp, acrid smell like gunpowder gone off, and an instant later he saw her. She lay across the trail, her body and mangled hands so still that he thought she was dead.

*Dear God in heaven, let her be alive.*

"Frederik!" Maureen shouted.

"Up here!"

*God in heaven*...Gott im himmel...Mein Gott im himmel. Somehow he couldn't get past the plea from so long ago—his own father's plea—held inside him.

Then Maureen was with them, listening with her ear against Katharina's chest. "She's breathing." She brushed hair back from the child's dirty face. "Come to, sweetheart. Please. *Please*. Frederik, help!"

Frederik looked at her blankly a moment, and then he felt his mind clear. *A blasting cap,* he thought. *Dynamite would have killed.* He picked up Katharina. "We'll get her to the hospital."

# TESSIE

My hard work with Mr. Stubner was paying off in orchestra. At the beginning of my junior year, I leapfrogged over other violinists so that now I was first stand, just one chair away from being concertmaster.

That position was held by a senior named Tran, who everybody liked. When he stood to play an A for the orchestra to tune to, he'd say, "Please." He led the violin section with a constant firmness that made us sound good. And sometimes when I turned a page of our music—the second person on a stand always got that job—he'd nod a thank you.

Kendall, on my left, was a different story altogether. She'd hoped to be concertmaster, expected to at least have my chair, and now she never looked at me without resentment showing.

I wasn't sure what to do about it, except act like I didn't notice, and when I knew she'd done something

like get top ratings in a music competition, I congratu-
lated her.

She rarely bothered to answer. Except once she said,
"How come you never enter anything? If you're not going to build a career, you shouldn't be taking up space
here."

"I don't think that's so," I told her. "Besides, my violin teacher says that preparing for competitions would divert me from working on the things I need to learn."

Kendall said, "Mr. Stubner has been teaching so long,
he doesn't know what the real world's like anymore. I
wouldn't have him for my teacher."

I said, "And maybe he wouldn't have you for his
student!"

After that, I gave up even saying "hi" to her.

She didn't talk to me, either, except to occasionally
whisper, just loud enough for one or two others to hear,
"Tess, you're playing sharp," or "Tess, would you count?
You're throwing me off!"

Ben told me, "Ignore her. She's jealous."

"She shouldn't be. She's a wonderful violinist."

"And a witch," he said. "You're crazy if you let her
get to you."

I never did find out if it was Kendall who told on Ben
and me. But someone did.

On the last Thursday of October, Ben and I cut
classes to wait in line for tickets to a live television show.
The tickets ran out before our turn came up, though, and

Ben and I ended the afternoon early. I went home in plenty of time to beat Mom there.

Only I found her waiting for me, still dressed up for work. "Why are you here?" I asked.

"I got a call from your school. Would you like to tell me about this special ensemble practice you and Ben had? None of your teachers seems to know anything about it."

I just stood there, caught too off guard to come up with an answer, feeling my face burn.

"I will not have you wrecking your future, throwing away all your effort and everything that's been done for you, for the sake of some teenage romance."

"But I'm not . . . We're not . . ."

"I don't want to hear it," she said, her voice brittle. "Just don't skip school again."

I stared at her, perplexed. That was all she was going to say?

And even more perplexing was how, for just an instant, her expression went soft and pleading, as if there was something that she really needed me to understand. "Tessie . . . ," she began.

She hadn't called me that in months—not since I'd made a scene about it—and I wondered what caused her to now.

She didn't finish her sentence. Fast as the odd moment had come, it was over, and Mom's voice and expression went brittle again. "I have to return to work," she said. "There's a letter for you on the table."

I read it after she left. It was actually one of two letters on the table: One was to her and one was to me, both from Dad.

Mine began, "Dear Tess, I have news to share."

I read quickly to the end, and then, my feelings in a turmoil of protest, I telephoned Montana. The clinic receptionist said, "Your father's in the middle of appointments, but I'll see if I can catch him. Can you hold?"

"Yes."

I held long enough to read Dad's letter several more times. He was going to get married again, to a woman with a nine-year-old daughter.

I was having a difficult time taking it in.

*No wonder Mom acted so odd,* I thought. She must have just gotten the same news, and even though she and Dad were divorced, nobody likes to be replaced.

"Tess?" I heard Dad's voice on the phone.

"I got your letter. Congratulations."

"Thank you."

"But, Dad, you're marrying somebody I don't even know."

"Not 'somebody,'" he said. "Her name is Meg. I wanted to tell you about her this summer when you two could have gotten to know each other in person, and when you could have gotten to know her daughter, Amy, too. Only you went to music camp instead of coming here, and then last week I got your note saying you're not going to make it out for Thanksgiving, either."

"I can't. I have a program. When are you getting married?" I asked.

"The week between Christmas and New Year's. We thought we'd get married in Hawaii and ask you and Amy to stand up with us. Will you be my best man?"

"I guess so," I said. "I don't know. I have to ask Mom. Hawaii?" Not that I cared where. It was just a question to ask when I suddenly couldn't trust myself to talk anymore.

Dad filled in details until he seemed to realize I wasn't really listening. "Look, Tess," he said. "I want..."

"It's okay," I told him. "Really. But I've got to go now. Really. Congratulations."

I said good-bye and put the phone down feeling kind of lost. And, I guess, scared, too, although at first I couldn't figure out why. Then I realized that up till now, *I* was the one who'd been doing all the changing. Even if I hadn't been going home very often, I'd always known home—and Dad—were there, just the way I'd left them. And now neither would ever be the same.

Mom gave me my Christmas present early: tickets for the two of us to holiday performances at Lincoln Center.

I looked at them—an opera, a ballet, a symphony concert. She'd even thrown in an evening at Carnegie Hall, which wasn't even a part of Lincoln Center. They'd be wonderful performances, and from the close-in seats she'd bought I'd be able to see faces and hear even the quietest, most individual sounds.

I told her, "Mom, I can't use these. Christmas week is when I go to Hawaii."

"I've been thinking about that trip," Mom said. "I don't see how you can make it. You've got SATs to study for and exams coming up in January. It's going to be hard enough for you to keep up on your violin, without your taking a week off from practicing."

"Dad's not going to understand."

"That depends on how you present it," Mom said. She handed me a piece of stationery and a pen. "I'll tell you what to say."

APPARENTLY MOM was right: Dad didn't argue, so he must have understood.

But I went to bed crying more nights than not, between then and Christmas. First I cried because I'd be missing the wedding. Then I cried because I was just as glad I wouldn't be at it. I cried because I might not like Meg and Amy. I cried because they might not like me.

I cried because I missed seeing Ben outside of school. Mom had begun telephoning me at four o'clock every day—just to say hi, she said, but I knew the real reason was to check up on me, and I cried about that.

I cried because I kept making mistakes in orchestra, and because I could guess from the pleased expression on Kendall's face that she thought we'd soon be switching seats.

I cried because Mr. Stubner asked why I'd begun playing like an automaton, without putting any of myself into my music.

I cried because half the people at school were snappish and pinch faced over one thing or another. The dancers were all either worn out from performances of *The Nutcracker,* or else they were upset at not having parts. The voice students and musicians who took private engagements were exhausted from doing holiday parties.

Teachers got provoked, and there was even a rumor that Gabriel Nageo, a senior flute player, had gotten fired by his flute teacher for not taking directions.

"I don't think teachers can fire you," I said, when some of us were talking about it after orchestra.

"No?" Kendall said. "Then you tell me why Gabriel's dropped out of school."

I didn't have an answer to that any more than I did to anything else.

I just knew I was miserable, and that it was at least partly because I'd been so rotten to Dad. I wondered if he'd ever forgive me.

I got my answer on Christmas Eve, when the apartment buzzer rang while Mom and I were eating dinner. A delivery man brought up a large insured box that Mom had to sign for.

When we opened it and took out layers of packing, we found a gift-wrapped present with a card that said, "Merry Christmas to my dearest daughter Tess, with love from your old man."

"I'm not going to wait for tomorrow," I told Mom. I could guess from the box and careful packing what my present just might be. With shaking hands I pulled off the ribbon and gift paper and opened the inner box and then the case inside. Dad had sent me a violin.

I peered through one of the instrument's f-shaped sound holes, read the label, and caught my breath. Dad must have been saving and saving for this. I'd expected to wait years for a violin so good.

I was so afraid to break even a string that I took forever tuning it. And then just as long examining the fine bow, tightening it, running rosin down it.

Cautiously I played a few short notes and then longer and fuller ones, not wanting to be disappointed. I was thrilled at the violin's rich tone. And when I finally dared play my best, I heard my best sound better than it ever had.

"Mom, did you know?" I asked.

"No. I wish he'd consulted me," Mom answered, setting her mouth in an unsmiling line. Then she added, "It's a lovely present." She gave it a speculative look. "You could start a career with that."

Mr. Stubner was as thrilled as I with my new violin. Not that it came as a surprise to him. I learned Dad had called him for advice.

He was less pleased, though, with how I played it that first lesson after holiday break. I'd gone hoping to surprise him with the start of a sonata I'd heard a fantastic violinist play at one of the holiday concerts Mom and I attended. At intermission I'd even bought one of the violinist's CDs so I could study just how she put so much emotion into each phrase.

I'd practiced and practiced, and when I played it for Mr. Stubner, I watched for his nod of approval. I wanted to see his pleasure and pride in me.

Instead I saw mirth.

"What's funny?" I asked.

He named the soloist I'd admired so much. "Right?"

"Yes."

"Tess, what you played was very nice, but it was her, not you."

"What do you mean?"

"The grief and anguish! Surely you can come up with something more honest than that."

"I thought it sounded honest," I said.

"It was when she played it, because she took a piece of music begun by a composer and finished it with skill and with what was inside her. But when you play, I want to hear what's inside *you*!"

"I don't think there's anything in there all that special," I told him.

"Well, well," Mr. Stubner said, smiling although his eyes looked sympathetic. "That is a problem, isn't it?"

I got in the last word, though, when I thought of it a few minutes later. I broke off in the middle of an exercise to say, "And the listener. The listener has something to do with how a piece of music is completed, too."

Mr. Stubner looked surprised. Then he said, "Right you are, Tess. And sometimes, the listener is the most important part, and the easiest part to forget."

THE REST OF January slid by in a blur of work and exams and tense, anxious faces. I didn't see my friends to talk to except at lunch, and then our conversations mostly ended up in our endless game of What If?

Even Ben got caught up in it: What if I'd started

playing/dancing/acting younger than I did? What if I'd
taken up a different instrument? Had a better teacher
early on? Been born with perfect pitch instead of just almost? Came from a family already in the music business?

When we weren't playing What If?, then we were on
to What's Next? We learned it from seniors stressing over
choosing between college and a music conservatory,
sweating out acceptances, applying for scholarships or
jobs, making frantic last efforts to stand out above super-
talented peers.

We had a third game, too, but it was one that we
mostly kept private. It was the game of What's After
That?

For some of us—the violinists and cellists and pi-
anists—who played solo instruments, a career as a concert soloist who traveled the world hung out there as the
biggest, brightest prize.

Others wanted a regular job with a good orchestra.
Sometimes I thought about that cellist I'd heard practicing the time Mom and I toured Lincoln Center, and I
wondered if he was doing what he wanted. I wondered if
maybe he'd rather be a concert soloist but didn't have the
personality to connect with audiences. You heard about
that, how some performers had a way about them and
others didn't.

And we all knew that some of us would be making a
career of teaching, either aiming for or drifting into it.
Growing into it, maybe. Teachers like Mr. Stubner had

done it all—had solo careers, played in orchestras and ensembles—and now were respected masters passing on their skill and knowledge.

But when I thought back to my first year in New York and the defeated orchestra teacher at that one school I briefly attended, I wondered which ones of us would end up like him.

I told Ben about him, and Ben surprised me by saying, "I've been thinking about teaching junior or senior high myself. I'd still have time to do some composing."

Then, looking a bit embarrassed, he said, "I like the idea of opening students' eyes to what music can be. The people who buy season tickets to symphony orchestras already know, and they're likely to see that their children do. But most kids—if they don't run into a good music teacher someplace, they might never find out."

All the What If? and What's Next? and What's After That? games left me mixed-up and feeling at odds with myself.

Sometimes I imagined myself as one of the lucky ones, a big-name soloist.

More often I just wished we could keep on right where we were, with nothing more changing except that the worried games would go away.

February came on wet and gray and with Mom and Mr. Stubner and me all pretty equally unhappy with each other.

Mom started it by deciding I should take part in a young artists' competition that had as its prize a guest appearance with one of Germany's finest orchestras. Auditions would be in April and the concert in June.

"Mom, that's not something I want to do. Not yet. I'm not good enough."

"Nonsense. Look where you sit in orchestra, one chair from concertmaster, a position you *will* win next year."

"I don't know that. And school's not a competition." I thought of Kendall. "At least not for most of us."

Mom's eyebrows arched. "Really?" she said, as though she knew exactly how we all ranked one another. It wasn't something we admitted doing, but these days the questions were always with us: Who was best and who was least promising and where everybody was in between.

"Please, Mom," I said, "I really don't want to enter a contest. You're going to be unhappy if I don't win, and if I do win...Mom, I'm not ready to play a real concert."

"That's really not for you to judge, is it?" Mom said.

"AND JUST WHO else should be the judge?" Ben asked. I'd expected him to be sympathetic, but instead he got almost angry. "Why don't you stand up to your mother? You're sixteen years old, but she runs your life like you're six."

"That's not fair," I told him. "Just because you're free to live like you want...Anyway, Mom's usually right. She's been behind almost every good thing that's happened with my violin. Without her, I wouldn't even be in New York."

A grin replaced Ben's scowl. "And you wouldn't have met me. So, okay, maybe your mom's ideas aren't all bad." His grin grew devilish. "Would a kiss make you feel better?"

"Not in the school cafeteria!"

"It's the only place I see you these days."

"You know Mom doesn't want me getting involved..."

"Back to her!" Ben jabbed a french fry into ketchup but didn't eat it. "Are you going to let her even decide how you feel?"

"No! It's just that things are complicated right now." I looked away so I wouldn't have to meet his eyes. "And I don't know if I'm ready to ... to get entangled."

"That's what I am?" Ben demanded. "An entanglement?"

I didn't answer, and a moment later, his voice calm again, Ben said, "Anyway, you ought to talk to your violin teacher about the competition. If he says no to your taking part, then your worries are over."

MR. STUBNER didn't say no. He said, "I don't think you should do it, Tess, but it's your decision."

"You can tell my mom it's a bad idea," I said.

"I did, when she called me about selecting music for you to prepare."

"Did she pick Vivaldi's Summer or did you?"

"His Four Seasons Concertos are lovely, sparkling music, and audiences are familiar with them. There's an advantage to playing music that people already like."

"But was Vivaldi her choice or yours?"

Mr. Stubner frowned, and I knew I'd gone too far. "I'm sorry," I said, opening the music. "I'll get to work."

IT DIDN'T TAKE me long to understand why Mr. Stubner disapproved of competitions. To prepare for this one, I had to let slide much of the other work he assigned me. I knew it frustrated him—I could see it on his face when he struggled to stay patient—but he helped me with the Vivaldi piece all he could.

Increasingly often, though, despite his patience, my lessons didn't go right. Sometimes he'd stop me in the middle of a passage and say, "No! This is beautiful music, Tess. I want you to give it the most beautiful sounds in your heart."

I'd nod as though to say, *Yes, I will.* The truth, though, was that I didn't have a clue how to find those sounds, and I worried that if I did find them, they might not be beautiful enough. It was safer to concentrate on being technically perfect. I knew how to work out fingerings and drill on hard passages until I could make them sound effortless, and I knew that would count in the competition.

Mr. Stubner listened and shook his head. "Being a good contest player isn't the same thing as being a good musician," he said.

But I couldn't aim for both at the same time. And I knew which I was supposed to be come April.

# TESS

The rain continues to soak the Rattlesnake through the rest of the afternoon, with each brief letup of sound followed by a new onslaught. Around suppertime, we finally see lighter skies to the west, but by then we've resigned ourselves to spending the night where we are.

"Tess," Amy says, "please get up with me to watch for the deer. Pop says it's okay if we carry pepper spray and stay in calling distance. Mom, too."

"How early?"

"They feed at first light."

"Before dawn? Once we're back home you can see deer any evening just by looking in people's gardens."

"It's not the same thing."

"But before *dawn*?"

"Please?"

LATER I LIE in my sleeping bag wondering how she talked me into agreeing. Maybe she did it by not taking no for an answer. Or maybe it had something to do with Midnight, because I'm sure she's still thinking about him a lot more than she lets on. I hope this will be an adventure that will somehow help her.

It occurs to me that might have been Dad's intention too, when he pointed out the meadow to Amy and said just enough to make her want to visit it in the early morning. *Dad,* I think, *is becoming an old softy.*

Amy whispers, "Are you asleep?"

"Almost."

"You forgot to tell me 'pleasant dreams.'"

"Pleasant dreams."

"Sametoyou," she says, making it one word. "Don't forget to set your watch alarm."

THE TENT IS still dark when we put on clothes we've kept warm in our sleeping bags. And then we're outside, giggling with excitement, finding our way through a wet forest that seems like a different place than it did in the day. The moon has gone down, but a scattering of stars shows swaying, black branches overhead, and our flashlight beams rove across looming, unidentifiable shapes.

Amy, treading on my heels, asks, "Are you scared?"

"No. Are you?"

"No." She pauses. "A little."

The meadow isn't far, and once there, we circle its edge until we're where the breeze won't carry our scent to any animals that come down to browse. I shake out the plastic sheet we've brought to sit on, and Amy decides where we should put it. She says, "Animals can't see us so well if we're *against* a tree instead of next to it. That's what Pop said, and also..."

"And also he told you we're not going to see anything unless we're quiet?"

"Yes."

I can sense her watching, intently scanning the dark field for all of a minute or two. Then she announces, "It's too early. We can talk till it's time."

"And how will we know when that is?" I ask.

Amy ignores the question. "Tell me about Ben," she says.

"I already have."

"Will he get a new girlfriend now?"

"I don't know." I hadn't thought of that. I hope not.

"There are lots of boys in Missoula you can go out with. And there are concerts you can be in, too, if you want."

"I don't think I ever want to go on another stage," I tell her.

"I know!" Amy says with feeling. "Before school was out, when my class put on a show, I had to be a tulip in a flower garden. It was so dumb." She squirms into a more comfortable position. "Did you want to be in that big concert where..." This time she doesn't finish "where you played so bad." She says, "...the one in Germany?"

"No."

"Then why did you do it?"

"Mom thought I should."

"She made you?"

"Sort of."

"How?"

"Well, she..." I halt, confused, unable to explain, and then I wonder if maybe the reason I can't explain is that that's not how it really was. Startled, I suddenly realize Mom didn't have any way to *make* me.

I remember how Mr. Stubner said that although he was against my entering the competition, the decision was mine. At the time, I thought he just meant that *he* didn't have the last word.

But maybe he meant that the decision really was up to *me*.

After all, even though Mom argued hard for it, I was the one who'd win or lose at the tryouts. All I had to do was not play my best there, and somebody else would have gone to Germany. I must have realized that, and yet I tried my hardest to win.

*But Mr. Stubner wouldn't want me to do less than my best.* So had he been suggesting that I was the one who had to say what was right for my playing?

I draw my breath in sharply, and Amy asks, "Do you hear something?"

"No."

I know what I want to believe—that the whole Germany thing was Mom's fault.

But what if it wasn't?

What if I'm the one to blame because I didn't have the courage to stand up for myself? I didn't listen to my own sense that I wasn't ready to play a big concert, and I didn't make anybody else listen to it, either. My heart starts pounding hard as I wonder if I could have, should have.

Amy tugs on my sleeve. "Are you paying attention? I said when I was a tulip, I had to wear a flower collar."

It takes me a moment to remember what she's talking about and to come up with a response. "Was it nice?"

"No. It was cardboard and it scratched. Did you wear a costume in your concert?"

I wonder how she pictures a concert. "Not a costume," I tell her. "I wore a formal, pearl-colored dress. It had a scooped neck and a long row of tiny buttons up the back."

Amy sighs, and her voice is wistful: "You must have been so gorgeous."

"I doubt that," I say. "Anyway, I was feeling too many other things to think about how I looked."

"Like what?" she asks.

I don't answer because I've heard something. Putting a hand out to shush her, I feel for my canister of pepper spray and then flick on my flashlight. Its beam catches the black and white slink of a skunk gliding to cover. Neither Amy nor I move—I think we hardly even breathe—until it's gone.

"Close," Amy says. Then she repeats her question. "Feeling what?"

"At the concert? Lots of things."

"I guess you were scared, huh?"

"Yes. I hadn't thought I'd be. Not too much. But when the orchestra was ready, waiting for me . . . when the conductor whispered, 'Fräulein' . . ."

I stop because my throat has become too tight for me to go on. Detail after detail is jamming into my mind, things I've been managing to forget.

Amy finds my hand and squeezes it. "It's okay," she says. "We should stop talking, anyway, or else the deer won't ever come."

She doesn't leave me anything to do but remember.

I wasn't sure what I had expected at the competition. Something more difficult, more like my audition for music school, maybe. Not that adrenalin didn't pump through me while I waited for my turn, or that I didn't feel a little sick, but some of that was good. It was how I felt when I had to play a piece for grades or in a school performance, and I'd learned that the tension in me added an edge to my playing.

I didn't know most of the other contestants because they came from all over. A couple were way out of their league and everyone was embarrassed for them. A few played really well. The more I heard, though, the more I knew I stood a good chance of winning if I just performed my piece the way I'd been practicing it.

And I did.

When the judges went to confer, I was pretty sure they would make their choice from among just three of us—a boy from another school, Kendall, and me.

I went to the ladies' room during the break before they announced their decision, and I was in one of the stalls when Kendall and her mother came into the bathroom. "Do you think I'll get it?" Kendall asked.

"The boy won't," her mother said. "But between you and Tess Thaler..."

"She doesn't deserve it," Kendall said. "She's never even entered a contest before, or played a guest spot anywhere."

"Then she'd better hope she doesn't win. A major concert isn't any place to find out if she's up to performing before a critical audience."

Kendall said, "If she does win, she'll mess up. She's been playing worse and worse all year, like half the time she doesn't know *what* she's doing."

TWO MONTHS later I was in Germany, rehearsing on the stage of a vast concert hall. I sounded the last note of my solo and lowered my violin, relieved that my first run-through with the orchestra had gone reasonably well. There'd been only a couple of places where my playing and that of the strings and harpsichord hadn't synced as well as they should.

"*Gut, fräulein. Gut,*" the conductor said. In the hall's fine acoustics, his words carried clipped and clear. They were accompanied by the light tapping of bows against music stands.

Pleased, I waited for the conductor to indicate which of the rough sections he wanted to tackle first. But instead he said, "Play as good this evening."

"I'll try my best," I answered, puzzled at his tone of dismissal. I glanced at the violin section and saw musicians already turning to other music. *Was that all the rehearsal I was going to get? And all that bow tapping—had it been applause because I'd played well or relief that I at least knew my part?*

PHONE CALLS HELPED me through the next crawling hours. I was glad the first one was from Dad. Mom, waiting at the hotel with me and as nervous as I was, had just been complaining about him. "Your father would have found a way to get over here if his new family weren't taking all his time."

"That's not fair," I'd told her. "It's not his fault the vet who was going to sub for him backed out."

Not for anything in the world would I have admitted how disappointed I was.

And Dad's first words were "I wish I could be there tonight."

"I wish you could be, too," I told him. And because he'd be hurt if I didn't say it, even though my stepmother and stepsister were still just faces in photographs, I added, "And Meg and Amy, also."

Next, Ben and then Mr. Stubner called. It was funny,

how alike they were in their attitudes about this concert. Neither thought I should be doing it, but both, I knew, were pulling for me with all their hearts.

"You ready?" Ben asked.

"I hope so. I didn't make any terrible mistakes at rehearsal, but there were places that needed more work. In that section where the tempo keeps changing, I came in too early once, and there was this one place where my part goes loud, only I went *too* loud, and..."

"Tess, you're going to be great," Ben said.

Mr. Stubner said, "Did I ever tell you that I made my debut in Germany?"

"No."

"I did, and now it's your turn." His voice got gruff. "You're one of the best students I've ever had, Tess. You know your piece. Be honest to what's inside you, remember who you're there for, and you'll be fine."

I LISTENED TO the first half of the concert from behind a side curtain, dazzled by the sight on the stage. The orchestra fanned out before the audience, violins to the left, violas in the middle, and cellos on the right. The polished metals and woods of flutes and clarinets, trumpets and French horns flashed in front of the percussion instruments lined up across the back.

*And now it's your turn.* Mr. Stubner's words kept repeating themselves in my mind. *My turn.* Like maybe I just had this one chance. I knew that wasn't what he meant, but I couldn't make the idea go away.

By the time the stage emptied for intermission, my hands were so sweaty I didn't know how I was going to hold my violin properly. And I felt like I might throw up.

A stagehand pointed to my mouth and drew a smile with his finger.

And then the string players and harpsichordist who'd play the Vivaldi concerto with me filed back out and took their seats.

I felt Mom straightening my dress, pale and shimmery and fitted to my shape except for a flare that began at my knees and went almost to the floor. Low-cut and sleeveless, the dress made me look twenty years old. Twenty-five, maybe. Grown-up.

Mom whispered last reminders, and then the conductor touched my arm. We needed to go now, me first, him right behind me.

I walked out quickly. *Command the stage.* Somewhere I'd heard that was important.

I paid my respects to the concertmaster. The musicians who had been wearing casual clothes that morning looked like different people now. The men were in tuxedos. The women's bare necks gleamed above matte black dresses. *They're all so elegant,* I thought. *And so assured. And so good. And they're going to accompany me?* All of a sudden it didn't make sense.

I didn't realize I'd halted until the concertmaster made a slight gesture. I turned then, quickly, into a spotlight that pinned me before an audience I couldn't see. I knew they were out there, though. That they were watching me, not a child prodigy in a recital but someone who looked like an adult. Someone they would expect to give a professional performance. Their welcoming applause became a smatter of claps and died out.

*"Fräulein?"* The conductor's soft question jerked me back to what I had to do.

I nodded. *Yes, I'm ready.*

From the corner of my eye, I saw him set a tempo. Then the strings swept into sound.

I tucked my violin against my neck. I raised my bow. I listened for my entrance. And then . . .

When Amy squeezes my hand again, the sky has already lightened to a deep color that I can't quite put a name to. Bluey charcoal, maybe, faintly glowing with the kind of half-light that plays tricks with your eyes. In the next minutes, time and again it plays the same trick with mine. I glimpse a shape at the edge of my vision and think it's alive, only to have it turn out to be a boulder or shrub.

Once, the glistening tops of the grass in front of me wave and part and then close back up, but the animal passing through stays hidden.

And then, just as Amy starts to say something, I hear a soft *snap* like a twig being stepped on. "Listen!" I whisper.

"To what?"

"I'm not sure."

Once more, a shape near the tree line seems to move, and this time I recognize the up-and-down lines of legs.

And then I make out the dark silhouette of a head and neck.

Amy clutches my arm as a large doe steps from the sheltering forest. The doe stops to listen and then moves farther into the meadow. Again she halts, and this time she makes a hoarse noise: a raspy sound like wind whistling up her throat.

And, suddenly, another doe and three fawns are in the clearing with her.

*Oh* ... I'm sure I just thought the word, but the lead doe looks my way alerted, ears cocked forward.

She takes a few stiff-legged steps toward us, stamps a hoof, and takes another step.

She blows air out her nostrils in a breathy snort, and the other deer lift their heads. And then the big doe turns and bounds into the forest, moving so quickly she seems to just disappear.

Right away, the others follow, all but the littlest fawn.

Confused, it steps this way and that and then runs toward us, halting a few feet away. It looks right at me.

I see its frightened eyes and its muscles too tense to move, and I hear the little animal make a sound of its own: a tiny, high-pitched *bleat.*

And then from the woods comes that snorting, breathy call again. The fawn leaps toward it, and the last glimpse I have is of the white underside of its small, flagging tail.

Amy whispers, "I was afraid he was going to get left. But did you hear him, Tess? Did you hear?"

"I heard," I answer, not trusting my voice to say more. I think of that scared *bleat* and picture how the little guy stood too frightened to move, too little to be alone. Tears fill my eyes.

They spill over, and in the damp, cool, mountain morning, I begin crying.

"What's wrong?" Amy asks.

"I don't know," I answer, choking a little laugh into the words. "I just need to cry."

"Okay," Amy says, and she sits with me while I cry and cry and cry.

As we walk back to our tent, Amy asks, "Why were you so sad? The fawn went back to its mother."

"I know it did. But for a moment it was so lost and so scared."

"And that's all?"

"I was thinking about some other things, too."

"What?"

"Mostly stuff I wish I could do over again. Do differently."

"The concert?"

"That's one of them."

"You're still glad you came here, aren't you?"

"That's been the best thing to come out of it."

Amy looks pleased. Then she asks, "But what was worst?"

"I guess the people I let down. In Germany and afterward. When I got to New York I didn't even call my violin teacher or Ben."

"You just left? You didn't say good-bye? How come?"

"I was ashamed. And also I knew if I was around them, I'd be around music, and I thought I wanted to get away from it. Only . . . Amy, I miss it so much." I try to make my voice light, but I'm only partly successful. "Sometimes I feel as lost as that fawn looked."

Amy studies me solemnly. "I knew you were crying for it."

She thinks awhile, and then she announces, as though she's just made a major decision, "If the fawn had needed me to, I'd have helped it. I wouldn't have let it down."

"I know that, sweetie," I tell her. "I don't doubt it for an instant."

"How about striking out on cross-country travel?" Dad asks after we're all up and packed. He and Meg are scrutinizing a trail-less section of topo map, looking for a shortcut that might regain us the day we lost to rain.

Meg answers, "One of my older maps shows a footpath. It's some distance away, but we could shoot for that."

The bushwhacking is rough going, with some hard climbing in places. We skitter down grab-onto-whatever-you-can descents knowing we're just going to have to go uphill again, and we lose an hour working our way around a large area of avalanche-downed pines. And when we do finally spot an ax-cut blaze high on a tree, we still have to look hard to find the trail it once marked.

All in all, it's one long, hard day of hiking that doesn't even allow a chance to talk. The payoff, though, is that by ten o'clock the next morning, we're above the gulch where Meg thinks the Bottners had their homestead. The upper end of it tapers out of sight into the high country, and where the gulch widens at the lower end, its floor appears to be an impenetrable mat of densely packed trees and dark undergrowth.

"What a place to try to live," Meg murmurs, as we begin our descent. Gesturing toward a rock outcropping on the somewhat barren hillside opposite, she adds, "That must be the rock ledge that the Randalls climbed up to."

We stow our gear at a camping spot a couple of hundred feet from the bank above Rattlesnake Creek, and Meg checks her vest pockets for her topo map and compass, pencils and notebook, tape measure, and camera. I'm wondering if she's going to do her exploration alone—feeling disappointed, because that's what it looks like—when she asks, "Tess, want to go along? I'd love some help."

"Sure," I answer. "I'll do whatever you want."

"I can help, too," Amy says, but Dad's ready with a different plan for her.

"I've got some plaster of paris for casting animal tracks," he says. "I thought you and I might set out along Rattlesnake Creek and see what we can find. Though I ought to warn you, we may need to wade right in."

Conflict races across Amy's face, and I hide a smile. I know exactly how she's feeling. It is so frustrating to want to do two things and have to pick one. The bag of casting material that Dad pulls from his pack wins her over.

MEG AND I head into thick growth along a runoff stream that funnels water into the gulch from the mountains. I ask what I should be looking for.

"Anything unnatural," she answers.

"Like apple trees or poplars?" I ask, remembering what she told me our first day out.

"Exactly. But also look for any kind of nonnatural debris—metal scraps, fencing, a can pile. Sawed lumber or shaped logs, of course. Leather—sometimes that survives a long time. And especially keep an eye out for odd ridges or depressions."

Meg rattles the list off so easily that I expect it will be just a matter of moments before we spot one thing or another.

We don't, and we're not successful when we climb to the rock outcropping hoping, as the Randalls did, that from up there we might notice some irregularity in the landscape.

Traversing our way down, we do come across a rusted can riddled with holes in a rough pattern, but there's no way of knowing if it was ever connected to any homestead in the gulch.

And Meg vetoes checking out a brush-filled, caved-in section of hillside that could be the remains of an old mine. "Too dangerous," she says. "It'd be nice to know, given Katharina's story about injuring her hands, but it will have to wait until a team can investigate in a way that won't risk a cave-in."

Back down in the gulch, Meg and I knock off for a midafternoon snack. Sounding disheartened, she says, "I really thought we'd come across *something* by now. I was so sure all the evidence pointed to this being where the Bottners lived."

"MEG?" I CALL. "Does rhubarb grow wild?"

"No!" Meg shouts, hurrying to me. "It does not!"

Leaning down, Meg peers at the plant's big leaves and scraggly stalks as though they're the most gorgeous things she's ever seen. She says, "In the old days this plant would have provided jellies and pies, protected against scurvy..." She pauses, looking around. "Assuming the Bottners did live here, then we're probably standing in their kitchen garden, which certainly would have been placed handy to the house."

She points out the area she thinks most likely to have contained the homestead buildings. "Let's work it in a grid, you taking one side and me the other. We'll walk up in one direction, return a couple of feet over, and so on."

"What about trees?"

"Go around them, but do your best to keep to the grid. And if you see anything...*anything*..."

I find the first confirmation that we really have found the homestead when my shirtsleeve snags on a twist of barbed wire protruding from a tree trunk. "Over here!" I yell. "Meg! I think I've found part of a fence!"

And thirty minutes later, still looking for more fence remnants, I trip and fall into a shallow depression hidden by rotting vegetation.

Meg gives me a hand up. Then, being careful not to move anything but leaves, we uncover the extent of the hollow. It's a square, roughly four feet on a side.

"What do you think it was?" I ask.

"It's too small to have been a root cellar," Meg answers, "so my best guess is that you've found the Bottners' outhouse!"

"You're kidding!"

"Hey! That's an important find!"

After that, the discoveries come quickly. We find mossy lines that Meg says are probably the cabin itself and that we'll come back to. She points to a spot where vegetation is particularly thick and guesses that's where the barnyard was. "I bet that if we dug under the sod, we'd find a rich layer of humus," she says. "Think cows, horses, chickens, mud, cow pies..."

And not far from that, a bed-sized rise covered with pine duff turns out to be a can pile. Junk pile, actually, where somebody threw stuff they didn't want. I ask Meg if she wants to go through it.

"Not now. Maybe when I come back with a follow-up team, but we'll probably just finish documenting the site and then leave things the way we find them."

"Why?"

"Because you destroy when you dig. Some future technology might let us learn something from all this that we couldn't now, and meanwhile, the site will be here to offer other people the thrill of discovery."

"And you just hope they won't cart things away," I say.

"You just hope," Meg agrees.

We trace the rest of the cabin's outline and then take a last break, sitting close to where Meg figures a porch might have been.

"I'm glad we'll be able to tell Katharina that we saw where she lived," I say. "Maybe, if you've got extra film, we could take some photos for her? Maybe of the way the mountains look from here? That must still be the same."

"That's a good idea," Meg says.

"I kind of feel like I know the Bottners," I say.

She nods. "A good day in the field often leaves me feeling as though I've met somebody. The thing is, no matter how much you study and investigate, when it comes to individual lives there are always things you just won't ever know."

I understand what she means. We know some of the facts of the Bottners' lives, and we've met Katharina, and

I've even held Frederik Bottner's fiddle. But we don't know what he thought about or talked about. All we even know of his music is that Katharina liked it and that it was good enough he could play for a country dance. Living out here, he probably never got a chance to study music seriously. I wonder if he ever wanted to.

I nudge a rock with my boot, uncovering a black bit of shaped wood that's different from the debris around it. Picking it up for a closer look, I notice how hard it is, and the way it's smooth and a bit concave on both sides...

"What do you have there?" Meg asks.

"I'm not sure," I say, showing it to her. "But I wonder... It almost looks like part of a violin peg."

Then I remember the violin Katharina showed us. How it had one peg different from the others.

"Meg," I say, "do you think...?"

As we leave the gulch, Meg asks, "So, how have you liked your foray into archaeology?"

"I've liked it," I answer.

"Enough to consider a career change?"

Laughing at her teasing tone, I answer, "No. But any summer you want help, you've got it."

She glances over at me. "So you've come to a decision?"

"Yeah."

"Have you told your dad?"

"That's next."

"No time like the present," she says, and when we find the others setting up tents, she tells Dad, "Amy and I can finish this. Why don't you and Tess fill the water bottles? You can get enough both for dinner and for our hike out tomorrow."

Filtering water is a slow process, and an extra set of hands makes it less awkward but no faster. Which, of course, is what Meg had in mind. *She's okay,* I think, wondering how I could have ever worried we might not get along.

I take a deep breath. "Dad, you said that when I wanted to talk..."

"I'd be ready to listen. I remember."

"I've been remembering, too, and thinking. Somehow I never put it all together before, how much you and Mom have done to give me a chance to become a really great violinist."

Dad makes a little dismissive motion with his hands. "Helping their kids is what parents do."

"Not all parents. Not like you have. Mom likes her museum work, but I need to know—if you didn't have my school expenses, would you cut down on your regular clinic work so you could do more rehab stuff?"

"And maybe let down that Lab pup the next time he needs patching together?" Dad says. "No way!" He sounds a little amused. "But surely all your thinking hasn't been about your mother and me?"

"No, but it was a starting place, and it's still important. But what I really want to tell you...I think I've finally got the concert figured out. What I didn't realize before is that even if I had no business being in it, it might have turned out okay if I'd remembered the real reason I was there."

Dad looks at me questioningly.

"It's something Mr. Stubner and I talked about once.

About music being a whole that's part composer, part musician, part listener. Only, when I got onstage, I forgot everybody but myself. I let down a entire hall full of people because I thought they'd come to hear *me.* They'd come to *hear,* and I was too wrapped up in myself to remember the difference."

"You probably didn't play nearly as badly as you think."

"No. Just not good enough."

Dad doesn't argue. He says, "You'd be the best judge of that."

"Which brings me to another thing," I say. "I think it's time I started making my own decisions. Because sometimes I do know what's best for me. And even if I can't be sure, I'm the one who has to live with the consequences." I glance at my father, who raises his eyebrows. "Of course," I add, "I may have some trouble selling that to Mom."

"Yep."

"So," I say, "what do you think?"

Dad caps off a filled water bottle and attaches the filter to an empty one before answering. "I think I'm about to learn that I'm going to lose my daughter again."

"It's not that I want to leave," I tell him. "I love being with you and Meg and Amy, and I love this place, too."

"But?"

"But I don't belong here the way I do in New York. The way my violin and I do. And if I don't go back, I may spend the rest of my life wondering about what might have been." I pause. "Are you disappointed?"

"I'm a little sad," Dad says, his voice thick. "But disappointed? No. I'm proud of you."

MEG IS PULLING out food when we get back. "Last-night-out menu," she announces. "I've set aside tomorrow's breakfast and lunch, and the rest is up for grabs."

It's a super meal, and the only bad thing is that this *is* our last night out. I'm not ready for our camping trip to end, and I don't think the others are, either. We drag out eating while Amy gives a detailed description of casting mink tracks, and then nobody moves to clean up.

We're drinking the end of the hot chocolate—Amy's is mixed with orange drink and lemonade—and talking over the day when we're startled by a harsh, falling scream. Alarmed, we look toward Rattlesnake Creek, where the sound came from. We hear it again, this time closer by.

"A mountain lion?" Meg asks, reaching for a canister of pepper spray.

"I'd say a hawk," Dad answers.

There's a sudden commotion in the brush just beyond us, and then we see that Dad was right. A big red-tailed hawk bursts out, flying right at us, and I duck. But then it hits the ground as though jerked back, and one wing splays out awkwardly.

We all move back, out of range of the bird's fury as it tries to get back in the air and fails. It tries and tries again and then makes one more, mighty effort. This time it manages to take off, half flying, half lunging into the forest, where it disappears.

Dad goes over to the torn-up ground where the bird struggled and picks up a length of fishing line. He swears, just one word. "It must have this stuff tangled around its wings."

"Do you think you can do anything?" Meg asks.

"It's worth a try," Dad says. "Although unless the bird injures itself too much to fly, I'll never be able to catch it."

"Do you want us to go with you?"

"No, you all stay here." Dad glances at Amy, who has her back to us, and I realize that he's thinking that if he does find the hawk, it's likely to be in bad shape.

After Dad leaves, Amy goes some distance away and sits down on a large boulder.

Meg, looking after her, says, "Poor kid. I wish she hadn't seen that."

We go about cleanup chores quietly, listening for sounds of Dad moving through the woods. Before he goes beyond earshot, we hear him skirting along one side of the gulch rather than going up its middle as we did. We also hear the hawk scream again, a loud cry that starts high and falls in pitch like a creature giving up.

We dry the dishes and are bundling up the food bag when Meg asks, "Tess, did you see where Amy went?"

I shake my head.

Meg calls, "Amy? Amy!"

When she doesn't get an answer, Meg calls again, more loudly. Then she tells me, "Start after your father. I'll check the creek and then catch up."

I take off at a run, calling out as I go. The forest is much more open up against the sparsely treed hillside, and I make such good time that soon I hear Dad yell back from above me.

I shout, "Do you have Amy?"

He shouts, "What?"

And then I hear Amy call from someplace off to his right, "I'm up here! I've got the hawk!"

I start to her. "Keep calling," I yell. "I can't see you."

"Here!" she shouts. "I'm up here!"

I get to her first. She's standing over the bird, which is on the ground, bleeding some and no longer struggling. Its eyes still flash angrily, though.

"You'd better stand back," I tell her.

"Why?" she asks. "It can't do anything." But she minds.

Moments later, Dad gets to us, and then Meg, who angles up from the other direction.

Using his sweatshirt and shirt as hand protectors, hood, and ties, Dad swiftly covers the bird's head and immobilizes its strong legs and taloned feet. Then, able to work safely, he examines a long tear on the bird's breast. "The cut's not deep, anyway," Dad says. "Probably got it falling into bushes."

Then he begins the delicate job of untangling fishing line. There are yards of it, wrapped around the hawk's wings, looped around its neck, caught between feathers. The bird tries to fight and then sinks back into stillness.

Finally Dad says, "I think I've got it all."

Amy, who's been watching intently, biting her lip, asks, "What will we do now?"

"Let's see if it can fly," Dad says. "I want all of you well out of its way." He swiftly frees the hawk and jumps back.

For a moment the bird continues to lie so still I wonder if it's died. But then I see its chest moving with its breath, and then a leg stretches out, toes extended, talons raking the air. It heaves itself upright and flails its wings. And then it's flying, a hesitant low flight that quickly turns into a wing-pumping climb and then, high above the ridge, into a current-riding glide. It screams its harsh, slurred cry one more time, only now it sounds like triumph.

"Oh!" I say, and I realize I've been holding my breath.

"Oh!" Amy echoes.

M eg, looking stern, waits for Amy's explanation.

Amy shows her a canister of pepper spray. "Pop forgot this. I wanted to take it to him."

"Why didn't you tell me?"

"Because you'd have taken it instead of letting me go." Amy's voice becomes a whisper, and her eyes plead. "I wanted to help Pop with the hawk. It needed a chance like we gave Midnight."

I see an unspoken signal go between Meg and Dad, and Dad says, "Amy, why don't you and I start back to camp?"

"Let's give them a few minutes," Meg tells me. "Your father will know what to say, both about her good intentions and about the risk she took running off alone."

"Dad's good at knowing what to say," I agree.

Only Dad's talk must not go quite the way we anticipate, because when Meg and I get back to camp we find Amy in angry tears. This time because of me.

"Pop says you're going back to New York," she says. "Are you?"

"Probably," I tell her.

"Then I hate you. You promised to stay."

For a moment she looks as if she's considering disappearing into the woods again, but she catches Meg's warning glance and goes only as far as the bank above Rattlesnake Creek.

"I'll go talk to her," I say.

"Hey," I say, dropping down next to her. "You don't really hate me, do you?"

"Yes. You promised."

"You know I didn't."

She sniffs. "Is your mom making you go?"

"No."

"Then *why*?" she demands. "If you can stay here, why don't you?"

"Because right now I belong where I can learn to be the best musician I can be."

She considers that and then asks, "But what if you mess up again?"

"I don't know," I answer. "I might. But you wouldn't want me not to try, would you? To have less courage than you showed tonight?"

"You mean taking the pepper spray to Pop?"

"No. I mean wanting to help the hawk even though

you knew it might die and make you sad like you were for Midnight. That was pretty brave."

Amy sniffs again. "I guess." She wipes her nose on her sleeve. "Mom got pretty mad at me."

"You scared her."

"Yeah." She looks sideways at me. "I don't really hate you."

"I know. And even after I leave, it won't be like we'll never see each other again. I'm going to come home every vacation from now on. And between vacations we can e-mail."

She asks, "Can I visit you in New York?"

"I'd love you to. I'll take you to school with me."

"Good!" Amy says. "I can meet Ben."

"Say," Dad calls, "is this a private conversation?"

"No, come on!" I call back.

He and Meg join us just as the evening sky deepens into the last shades of twilight.

We spend a few minutes planning our hike home and then we grow quiet as two owls begin calling to each other across the gulch. I'm about to try answering them when a muted splash alerts us to the dark shape of a beaver gliding through the water below. Suddenly it dives from sight, its tail slapping hard against the water and making a loud *thwack* that cracks the air.

I don't know which of us say, "Wow!" Maybe all of us. I add, "I've never heard that before."

———

THE DAY after we come out of the woods, I begin preparations for my return to New York. Not that I will go right away—I've decided to spend the rest of the summer with Dad, Meg, and Amy. But I have to let everyone know what I'm doing.

Mom, when I call her, says, "I knew you'd come to your senses. I'll telephone Mr. Stubner."

"Please don't," I tell her. "I'd like to start handling more things like that for myself." Then I add, "And I'd like to start deciding more things for myself, too, especially about my music."

"We'll see," she says. "When the time comes—"

"Mom, the time already came, only I didn't know it. From now on, some things really do have to be different."

I wait to hear if I'm asking to return on terms Mom won't accept. I can imagine her saying, *If that's what you're expecting, you'd better stay where you are.*

But instead, after a long, long pause, she says, "We'll work things out, Tess. Together." Then she adds, "I've missed you."

I call Mr. Stubner next. He tells me to enjoy my holiday and please bring him back a quart of huckleberries. He's always wanted to try some.

Ben's and my conversations are private. We have so many that I have to put in some hours at the clinic to pay for my share. And Ben calls me even more than I call him. He hasn't gotten another girlfriend. He wants to see

me in my pearl-colored, shape-fitting formal. He's working on a new composition that he's going to call "Tess."

I think Amy's forgotten about wanting violin lessons,
which is probably just as well. Drums, I'm thinking, might
be more her style. Anyway, she's on to a new project. After
I buy my phone card, Amy and I spend four dollars of
our joint kennel-cleaning earnings on ice-cream cones,
and we put the rest in a jar she labels, TRIP TO NEW YORK.

Of all the things I'm doing, though, what I enjoy the
most is playing my violin again. And every time I play it,
I become more certain that I've made the right choice,
even though I don't know where my choice will eventually lead.

The morning I take my violin out to the nursing
home, Meg and I walk in to find at least thirty people
gathered in the activity room. Mostly they're nursing-
home residents, but Dad and Amy are there, and also Mr.
and Mrs. Dreyden, whom I've invited. I give my old violin teacher a big hug. And I hug Mrs. Armitage, who accompanied me at my first recital. I invited her to be a
guest, but she said she'd rather accompany me again.

One of the nurses tells me, "We thought Katharina
understood that it was you who'd be here, but for the last
hour she's been telling everyone her father was coming to
play."

Katharina, though, looks at me with only the briefest
flicker of puzzlement before her face clears. She says, "I
knew you'd come back."

"Meg and I have lots to tell you," I say. "We found where you used to live and we've brought you pictures. But first, would you like to hear some music?"

"I wouldn't be out here if I didn't," she answers.

I begin with several old melodies that I think the nursing-home residents might know, and I'm pleased to see feet tapping and even a few people singing.

Katharina listens with pleasure lighting her face, and when I stop, she says, "Just like Papa. I always did like his music best."

"I'll end," I say, "with a rather long piece. It's the violin concerto called Summer, by composer Antonio Vivaldi."

I nod to Mrs. Armitage, pull my bow in the first downstroke, and hear the first note go out just right. And then I'm off and flying through the concerto's marvelous beginning.

And even though I'm caught up in the sound, some part of me is aware that my audience is caught up with me. I can feel my music reaching out to them, and, closing my eyes, I know that's exactly how I want it.

# FREDERIK
## 1918

You want help with the dishes?" Frederik asked.

"No," Maureen answered. "You go on reading the paper. Anything special in it?"

"War news." He scanned the front-page stories, his feelings mixed as they always were when he thought about the war with Germany. He and Maureen were doing all they could to grow food for America's soldiers, but Frederik wished the fight was with a different enemy. After all, his father had been born in Germany, and both of Frederik's uncles. In fact, as far as Frederik knew, his uncle Conrad still lived in Munich.

Frederik hadn't heard from him after the round of letters the year Frederik's father died. The war had put him in Frederik's mind again, though, and Frederik hoped he was all right.

Sometimes Frederik wondered about the decision he'd made that summer; where he'd be now if he'd chosen to go to his uncle Conrad instead of coming here.

Maybe he'd be a German soldier? But, no, Frederik
didn't believe that. The United States would always be
his country, and he couldn't imagine ever betraying it.
No more than he could imagine having any wife other
than Maureen or any daughter other than Katharina.

Still, it gave a body pause to think how just one decision, made differently, might have changed his whole life
and the lives of others, too. And he'd had to make it
when he was just a kid!

If he'd gone to live with his uncle Conrad, he'd never
even have met Maureen. But of course, while some of
the best parts of his life wouldn't have happened, some
of the worst parts wouldn't have, either.

Frederik again heard in his mind the sharp crack of
the blasting cap that Katharina had found and somehow
set off. In the two years since, he'd come to realize the
sound would always be a part of him, as vivid as his memory of bringing her home from the hospital afterward.

They'd sat up with her all night, trying to ease her
when she whimpered or cried out, and toward dawn,
Maureen had asked Frederik to get out his violin.

"I couldn't play," he'd said. "The last thing I want is
music."

The look Maureen had returned had been long and
measuring. "Since when," she'd asked, "did you start playing just for yourself?"

Now her voice brought him back to the present. "If

you're just daydreaming over that paper, how about getting out your fiddle?"

"I'll be glad to," he answered.

*Fiddle,* he thought, smiling. *Uncle Conrad being a music professor, he'd have probably wanted it called a violin. Or whatever the German word for* violin *is.* And he'd surely have taught Frederik to play a different kind of music than Frederik had taught himself.

Frederik tuned his instrument as he walked outside, A string first. He turned the next peg and felt it crack, and his D string went from taut to slack. *"Ahhh!"* he exclaimed. "No!"

Katharina, playing on the porch, asked, "What's wrong?"

"A tuning peg has split down the middle."

"Can you fix it?"

"I guess I'll have to make another."

"And then will you play?" she asked.

"I'm going to have to do that, too, since I have requests from both members of my best audience!"

"That's me and Mama, right?" Katharina asked.

"That's you and your mother," he agreed.


WHILE FREDERIK whittled a new peg, he thought about how much his daughter loved music and how he wished he could teach her to play his violin. But with her hands the way they were, that would never happen.

The best he could do was play for her when she asked.

It was growing dark by the time he finished whittling and sanding. Maureen brought out a kerosene lamp so he could see to position the new peg and run the D string through and around it. He tuned, tested, and then announced, "It's holding! What music should we break it in with?"

"A waltz," Maureen suggested.

"Something fast," Katharina said.

From farther up the gulch came the first, tentative call of an owl. *Hooo hoooo.*

"No. Wait!" Katharina said. "Can you answer him?"

Frederik blew out the light, tucked the violin to his neck, raised his bow, and listened.

The call came again. *Hoo hoo-hoo hooo hoooo.*

"I can try," Frederik said. Lightly touching the lowest string, he began playing a gentle harmonic, haunting and soft as the night.

## ACKNOWLEDGMENTS

My sincere gratitude for help with this book goes to many:

To the educators and students who provided insight into the lives of gifted young people striving for excellence. I'm especially indebted to Mindy Chermak and Anne Dykstra of New York City's Professional Performing Arts School; to the students there who talked with me about their hopes and worries and about how they thought Tess might feel and might meet a crisis; to Roberta Kosse and John Tucker of the Professional Children's School in New York; and to Andrew Thomas of the Juilliard School.

To violinist Margaret Nichols Baldridge and to Joseph Henry, director of the Missoula Symphony Orchestra.

To U.S. Forest Service foresters and historians Mary Horstman, Milo McLeod, and David Stack for sharing their knowledge of Rattlesnake history and their enthusiasm for historical archaeology.

To the helpful staffs of the Montana Historical Society Library, the Missoula Public Library, and the University of Montana Mansfield Library, and particularly to the Mansfield's retired archivist, Missoula historian Dale Johnson.

To longtime Montanans Bud and Janet Moore for talking with me about trapping, to biologist Dr. Richard Hutto of the University of Montana for answering my questions about hummingbirds, and to bird rehabilitator Kate Davis of Raptors of the Rockies for helping me see Midnight.

To my faithful (and persevering) writing buddies, Peggy Christian, Sneed Collard III, Hanneke Ippisch, Wendy Norgaard, Dorothy Hinshaw Patent, and Bruce Weide.

To my family, especially to Carie, Troy, and my husband, Kurt, for a memorable camping trip that began with ascending the Rattlesnake's Stuart Peak. To my son, Kurt, for keeping Montana's beauty before me.

And to three special people: my editors, Diane D'Andrade, who glimpsed the book I wanted to write, and Michael Stearns, who helped me find a way to write it; and my agent, Elizabeth Harding, who stayed with me through each step.

## Music and Musicians

### BOOKS

Feldman, David Henry, and Lynn T. Goldsmith. *Nature's Gambit: Child Prodigies and the Development of Human Potential.* New York: Basic Books, 1986.

Goulding, Phil G. *Classical Music: The 50 Greatest Composers and Their 1,000 Greatest Works.* New York: Fawcett Columbine, 1992.

Hoffman, Miles. *The NPR Classical Music Companion: Terms and Concepts from A to Z.* Boston: Houghton Mifflin, 1997.

Kenneson, Claude. *Musical Prodigies: Perilous Journeys, Remarkable Lives.* Portland, Ore.: Amadeus Press, 1998.

Stern, Isaac, and Chaim Potok. *My First 79 Years.* New York: Knopf, 1999.

Winner, Ellen. *Gifted Children: Myths and Realities.* New York: Basic Books, 1996.

## INTERNET SOURCES

*Lincoln Center for the Performing Arts.*
www.lincolncenter.org
*MENC: The National Association for Music Education.*
www.menc.org
*Symphony Orchestra Institute.* www.soi.org

## Montana History and Archaeology

### BOOKS

Cohen, Stan. *Missoula County Images, Vol. II.* Missoula, Mont.: Pictorial Histories, 1993.

Farr, William E., and K. Ross Tools. *Montana Images of the Past.* Boulder, Colo.: Pruett Publishing Co., 1978.

Koelbel, Lenora. *Missoula the Way It Was: A Portrait of an Early Western Town.* Missoula, Mont.: Gateway Printing & Litho, 1972.

Moore, Bud. *The Lochsa Story: Land Ethics in the Bitter-root Mountains.* Missoula, Mont.: Mountain Press, 1996.

Poe, Forrest, and Flossie Galland-Poe. *Born in Rattlesnake Canyon: An Oral History of the Rattlesnake Valley 1910–1940.* Edited by Mark Ratledge. Missoula, Mont.: Birch Creek Press, 1992.

Spritzer, Don. *Roadside History of Montana.* Missoula, Mont.: Mountain Press, 1999.

## INTERNET SOURCES

*Society for American Archaeology.* www.saa.org
*Society for Historical Archaeology.* www.sha.org
*USDA Forest Service Passport in Time Volunteer*
  *Archaeology and Historic Preservation Program.*
  www.passportintime.com